SWAMPLAND EMPIRE

Riley Rand arrives in Blue Lake Valley, announces he owns the entire area, and will be bringing a herd of cattle to take possession. But some of the residents don't take too kindly to the news...

Wayne D. Overholser, winner of three Spur Awards from the Western Writers of America, leaves his usual spell of excitement and emotion in this fast paced tale of the Wild West.

SWAMPLAND EMPIRE

by

Wayne D. Overholser

The Golden West Large Print Books
Long Preston, North Yorkshire,
BD23 4ND, England.

British Library Cataloguing in Publication Data.

Overholser, Wayne D.
    Swampland empire.

    A catalogue record of this book is
    available from the British Library

    ISBN   978-1-84262-936-9 pbk

Published in Large Print 2013 by arrangement with
Golden West Literary Agency

The Golden West Large Print is an imprint of Library Magna
Books Ltd.

Printed and bound in Great Britain by
T.J. (International) Ltd., Cornwall, PL28 8RW

Chapter One

The town of Getalong was in Blue Lake Valley far down in the southeast corner of Oregon, but there wasn't a map in existence that showed it. The reason was simple. The map makers had never heard of it, for Getalong was less than a year old on this June day when Brad Wilder drove Cory Steele's wagon into town for supplies.

Brad had been whistling all the way in from the Steele place. He felt good, and he had a right to. Given two more years, or even one, and he'd be set. Then he was close enough to the store to recognize the two saddle horses racked in front, and the good humor in him died. One belonged to Whang Dollit, the other to Nick Bailey.

Brad pulled up in front of the store, gray eyes on the saloon door. Even a new country was likely to have its share of tough hands, and Whang Dollit filled the bill here. Not that he claimed to be tough. He didn't have to. It was written all over him, and some of that writing had rubbed off on young Bailey.

Brad tied the team, and went into the store. It was empty. Dollit and Bailey would be in the saloon. He went on along the rough pine counter to the back room, hoping he would find Tom Hildreth, the store owner, there. Before he had thrown in with Cory Steele and the wagon train a year ago, Brad would have gone out of his way to get into a fight just for the joy of the fighting, but this year had changed him. Cory had done that, Cory and his dark-eyed daughter, Jeanie.

Hildreth wasn't in the back room, so he'd have to be in the saloon. Brad walked back to the front door, hoping that Hildreth would hear him. He stood there for a time, looking across the valley, and for a moment he forgot Whang Dollit. Blue Lake Valley had everything that went into the making of a good cattle country – grass.

The worst thing about this country was the distance to a settlement, for it was stretching the truth a little to call Getalong a town. There was this one two-story building. The first floor consisted of the store on one side, a saloon on the other; the second was a single large room where the settlers held their dances. A shed stood behind the building, some corrals beside it, and there was a dwelling house to the east. That was Getalong, and Tom Hildreth owned it all.

Impatience grew in Brad. He swung back, and walked through the wall door into the saloon side of the building. He had no reason to think he'd have trouble with Dollit today, but sooner or later it would come. His dislike of the man was instinctive, and he had no illusion about how Dollit felt toward him.

Dollit and Nick Bailey were bellied up against the bar, two pine planks laid across a couple of whisky barrels. Hildreth stood behind the bar, a fat man with a shiny bald head and a great white beard that gave him the appearance of a benign Santa Claus. In a way he was exactly that, for he was giving credit to every settler in the valley except Cory Steele and Whang Dollit.

Hildreth said in his friendly way: 'Howdy, Brad. This your drinking day?'

'No. I've got a list of stuff Jeanie wants.'

Dollit grinned and winked at Hildreth. 'I hear Jeanie don't like a man that drinks.'

He was a squat man, a head shorter than Brad and fifty pounds heavier with a dark-jowled face that was always barren of good nature, even when he grinned as he was doing now. Whang Dollit's smiles never reached up into his eyes that were as black and shiny as chipped obsidian.

'Dollit,' Brad said evenly, 'you must have quite a time living with yourself.'

'Cut it out,' Hildreth broke in. 'I'll get your stuff, Brad.'

'No hurry, is there?' Dollit asked. 'I've got a notion Nick here wants to say something.'

Bailey had been staring at an empty whisky glass in his hand. He raised bloodshot eyes to Brad, scowling, then dropped his gaze again to his glass. 'Not today, Whang.'

'Why this is as good a day as any,' Dollit said. 'You need another drink.' He reached for the bottle, and filled Bailey's glass. 'A man who's losing his girl has got to keep his courage up.'

'Cut it out, Dollit,' Hildreth said again. 'Go ahead with your drinking. I'll go fix Brad up.'

'Slow down, Tom,' Dollit said. 'You're too fat to be hurrying around like this. Bad for your heart.' He lifted paper and tobacco from his shirt pocket, gaze swinging to Brad. 'Heard the news?'

Brad held his answer a moment, watching Bailey who was slowly turning his filled glass between thumb and forefinger. He was twenty-three, and more of a kid than he should have been at that age. Slender, high-strung, nervous, Nick Bailey was the kind who might blow up without warning. Now, filled with whisky and with Dollit's words honing his jealousy to a fine edge, he might do the unexpected.

Dollit's big hands fisted. He said omin-

9

ously: 'I asked you a question, Wilder.'

Still watching Bailey, Brad said: 'No, I ain't heard no news.'

'Well, there's news to hear, bucko,' Dollit said as if pleased by the opportunity to tell it. 'Just like I've been saying. A man ought to be sure that a piece of land is open for filing before he settles on it. You fools went along with Cory Steele with your eyes shut. Now you'll lose your places just like I figured.'

'Well, what is this news?' Brad asked.

'What have I been saying all winter? I kept telling you this here valley had been taken over by the state as swampland. Now it's been sold to a cowman named Riley Rand. Where does that leave you and Cory Steele and the rest?'

'Where does it leave you,' Brad demanded, 'providing it's true?'

'It's true, all right,' Dollit said with deep satisfaction. 'I talked to Rand. His herd's down the trail, but he's in the valley. Camped below the south rim. He wasn't pleased when he got a look at our shacks. No, sir, he sure wasn't. Claims he bought fifty thousand acres, and that's all there is in this valley.'

'Fifty thousand acres,' Brad said slowly. 'What kind of a cussed lie are you passing out, Dollit? There ain't five thousand acres of real swampland around the lake.'

'No, there ain't,' Dollit agreed, 'but that don't make no never mind to the state or Riley Rand. The state wants a dollar and a quarter an acre, and Rand wants the range. He showed me an official map. The whole valley, tules and sagebrush and all, is marked with red S's. It's been called swampland whether it's swamp or not, and he's got it.'

Brad shoved his hat back with a thumb, glancing at Hildreth who was staring at Dollit as if uncertain whether to believe this or not. It could be true, for there had been similar rumors almost from the day the wagon train had reached the valley.

Cory Steele knew, as all of them knew, that large pieces of land in this part of Oregon had been turned over to the state by the federal government as swampland. The state, in turn, was selling it to cowmen who were driving their herds north from Nevada and California, but Cory had pointed out that at this late date anyone who wanted free land had to gamble.

The bulk of the good land had been homesteaded long ago. If a poor man wanted a home, he had to take what Uncle Sam had left to give. The valley was isolated, but there was water here, and in time a railroad would come. Or if it didn't, cattle could be pooled and driven south to the railroad at Winnemucca.

So, because Cory Steele was a persuasive man, they had gambled; they had built their cabins and turned their cattle into the lush grass around the lake and along the creek.

'You settled here, too,' Brad said finally. 'I asked where it left *you?*'

Dollit laughed. 'Well, sir, I ain't worrying. I'll make some money. The way I look at it, we've got a little nuisance value, so I figure to hang and rattle until this Rand makes us a proposition.'

'What kind of a proposition?' Hildreth asked.

'Hell, how would I know? I'll get something, though. Rand will have to send for a U.S. marshal to run us out. I figure it'll be cheaper if he buys us out just to get rid of us.'

'Wouldn't be much,' Hildreth said thoughtfully.

'No, but it'd be something.'

'Not for anybody who planned to make a home here,' Brad said curtly. 'You gonna get me this stuff, Tom?'

'Sure, right away,' Hildreth said. He turned and moved ponderously into the store.

Brad followed, and handed him the list Jeanie had made out. Hildreth scanned it. He shook his head. 'I'm plumb out of canned tomatoes, Brad. I've got everything else.'

'Then I guess she'll do without tomatoes.'

'I sent a wagon out early in the spring,' Hildreth said apologetically. 'It ought to be in before long. How is Cory, Brad? I ain't heard lately.'

'Poorly,' Brad said. 'It's been two months

since that ornery cayuse threw him, but his leg ain't mending like it should, and he's got an appetite like a bird. Jeanie thought some tomatoes would go down pretty good.'

'I'm sure sorry, Brad. I just ain't got a can.'

Brad carried the supplies to the wagon as Hildreth set them out, and, when he was finished, he tossed a gold eagle on the counter. He asked: 'You believe what Dollit said about this Riley Rand?'

Hildreth drew some silver dollars from his pocket and laid three of them down. 'I'm afraid I do, Brad. He ain't got any reason for lying.'

Brad pocketed the silver, thinking of Dollit who had drifted into the valley the fall after the wagon train had come. He had built a cabin, and that was all he had done. He had not put in a garden; he didn't own any cattle or chickens or pigs. Just a saddle horse and a pack animal, but he seemed to have money.

Until he had taken up with Nick Bailey, Dollit had been a friendless man, largely because he jeered at everyone for settling here.

From the first he had prophesied the very thing he now said had happened. According to the gossip, he was on the dodge and the valley was a good place to stay for there was no lawman within a hundred miles. Now Brad wondered.

'I dunno,' Brad said. 'He's a scheming son-of-a-bitch. Maybe he's figured out something else.'

'Maybe.' Hildreth put his hands on the counter and leaned across it. 'Brad, that Bailey boy worries me. He's drinking too much. Is it Jeanie?'

'Don't ask me,' Brad said irritably. 'He's got as much chance with her as anybody.'

'Except that you're Cory's neighbor, and you've been helping 'em. Nick's been worse since Cory busted his leg.'

'Well, what do you expect me to do, tell Jeanie to marry him?'

Hildreth shook his head. 'No, but somebody's got do something. He's been in love with her for a long time, Brad. He figures he's lost Jeanie, and he blames you.' The store

15

man gestured wearily. 'Me, I blame Cory. He never liked Nick much. I've been thinking you might talk to Cory. Have him give the boy work. Have Jeanie invite him out for a meal. Do something before Nick goes plumb loco.'

'I'll tell Cory,' Brad said, and, turning, walked out.

Without intending to, Jeanie Steele made a man's heart do things. Brad and young Bailey weren't the only men in the valley who were in love with her, and Brad wasn't sure he had the inside track. He knew that Cory liked him, but that didn't help with Jeanie. She wasn't the kind who could be told by her father or anyone else who she had to marry.

Brad paused in front of the store to roll a smoke, his eyes on the long ridges of the Blue Mountains to the north as he thought of the first time he had seen Jeanie. He had been aimlessly riding north from Linkville along the east side of the Cascade Mountains, a drifter at twenty-five without a solid thought in his head. He had turned west to follow the Santiam Pass to the Willamette Valley when he had met the wagon train. Jeanie was riding with Cory up in front, a slim, dark-haired girl with a scattering of freckles across a pert nose and eager brown eyes that danced with anticipation.

Brad had never thought it would happen to him, this thing of falling in love with a girl the first time he saw her, but it had. He could have had his choice of a hundred girls. Brad Wilder had a way with girls, and he'd had little conscience about it. He'd taken them to dances, they'd flirted with him, he'd kissed them, and he'd ridden off without a second thought about the broken hearts that lay along his back trail. Then he'd seen Jeanie, and the pattern had been reversed.

They had camped that night on the Deschutes. He had sat up late with Cory Steele after the others had gone to bed, and he had listened to Cory talk about the future of Blue Lake Valley. Cory had seen it when he had come out this way a short time before, and, when he had gone back across the Cascades, he had sold everything he owned and talked his neighbors into coming with him.

'Look at you, Wilder,' Cory had said. 'You don't own nothing but a buckskin horse and a saddle and the clothes on your back. Where are you headed?'

'Why, I never thought much about it,' Brad had answered.

'Then you'd better start thinking. A man shouldn't wait till it's too late to decide on what he's shooting at. I came near doing that. Tomorrow we're swinging over to the Crooked River to pick up a herd I bargained for. We ain't gonna farm. The season's too short, but we'll work our cattle together, and we'll drive to market together. We can use a young buck like you who's not afraid of work. How about coming along?'

'I'm broke,' Brad had said. 'I wouldn't fit.'

Cory had laughed then. 'Sure you'll fit. I'll loan you enough to get started. Don't ask me why except that I kind of cotton to you. I'll give you all the time you need to pay me back. It's a chance of a lifetime, I tell you.'

'Let me sleep on it,' Brad had said.

So he'd slept on it, and he'd dreamed about Jeanie. When he woke, there was Jeanie bending over a campfire, talking with Cory and laughing, a trim, supple girl who had gathered into her slim body and sharp mind everything that Brad Wilder had ever wanted in a woman. Ten minutes later he had told Cory he'd go along.

Now he fired his cigarette and flipped the charred matchstick into the dust. He hadn't told Jeanie he loved her, mostly because he was head over heels in debt to Cory. Perhaps it was false pride. He wasn't sure, but he wanted things to be right when he proposed.

He untied the team, and stepped into the wagon seat, thinking it was a great note for Tom Hildreth to tell him to ask Cory to encourage Nick Bailey. Well, he'd do it because he'd promised Hildreth, but it would be a waste of breath.

'Wilder.'

It was young Bailey, standing in the saloon

door. Brad said: 'Well?'

Bailey came out of the saloon, reeling a little, and grabbed the hitch rail. He said, thick-lipped: 'I've got something to say now, Wilder. You stay away from my girl.'

'I'll stay away from Jeanie when she tells me to,' Brad said. 'Not before.'

'I'm telling you to!' Bailey shouted. 'She's my girl. We're engaged. We're gonna be married. Savvy?'

'You can go to the devil,' Brad said, and drove away, leaving Bailey hanging to the hitch rail and cursing him in a blurred drunken voice.

Brad followed the wheel ruts made by Cory Steele and the other settlers who lived south of Getalong. A mile from the store the ruts turned east, keeping to the dry sage flat above the lake that lay to Brad's right, a blue center of a green oasis. Tules crowded the shore, acres of swampland that Cory Steele swore he would drain someday and then he'd have the best grass land in the state, but that day was far ahead. It would take time, and now Brad wondered if there was any.

There were two worlds here, one surrounding the other. The desert lay all around, drab and gray even now in June. The rattle of Brad's wagon stirred a band of antelope into flight away from the road. Young hawks in a nest under a sagebrush clump showed their youthful belligerance as Brad passed, and somewhere off to his left a meadowlark gave out its sweet song.

The other was a water world of lake and swamp, of tules and coon-tails and willows, and grass that by fall would be high enough to hide a calf. Here were the bragging trumpeter swans, pelicans and egrets, herons and ducks and geese. Kildeers rose in front of Brad's wagon and fled, calling out plaintively.

There was a third world, too. It was twenty miles away. That was the high country of the Steens Mountains to the south and the Blue Mountains to the north, summer range for all the cows that the settlers would ever own. The first day Brad had seen this country he had understood why Cory Steele had brought his people here, why he'd told Brad that night that here was their big opportunity.

For the first time since he had come to the valley, Brad was not stirred by this land, and, for the first time, he found himself doubting Cory's judgment. It would be a cruel thing to bring people here, encourage them to build their cabins and make their homes and dream their dreams, and then have everything taken from them. Cory would not knowingly do anything that was cruel. Brad did not question his intentions, but on the other hand he could not help questioning his judgment – if what Whang Dollit was telling was the truth.

Brad passed old Rimrock O'Shay's cabin and waved to him, passed the Widow Bain's place and waved to her. They were typical of the people Cory had brought to the valley. They had believed in Cory Steele just as Brad had believed. To them Blue Lake Valley had become a Promised Land. Anger began to burn in Brad as he thought of this.

As Tom Hildreth had said, there seemed to be no reason for Whang Dollit to lie.

In early afternoon, Brad came to the place that was set on a grass-covered bench above the lake. It testified to Cory's wealth just as did the fact that he paid cash to Hildreth for everything he bought. It was the only cabin in the valley that had more than one room. There was one large room across the front that faced the lake. The rear half was divided between the kitchen and Jeanie's bedroom.

Jeanie had seen him coming. She stepped out of the kitchen door and waved to him, her full lips smiling. When he pulled up, she came up to the wagon.

'Get the tomatoes?' she asked.

He sat motionless, his eyes on her. She was something of a tomboy who could ride any horse in the valley; she liked to hunt, and she was a good shot. Because she was honest and inherently good, he wondered if she knew what she had done to Nick Bailey and every single man in the valley, including Brad.

'You know you're as pretty as a new red-wheeled buggy, don't you?' Brad asked.

Stepping back, she put her hands on her slim hips and frowned reprovingly. 'You didn't stay in Tom's store like I told you, did you?'

'Why?'

'It would take some of his whisky to put that blarney on your tongue,' she said sternly. 'Now did you or did you not get the tomatoes?'

'No. Hildreth didn't have any. He says he's got some coming.'

'Coming!' she cried. 'What good will that do? Dad needs...' She stopped. 'Well, that's what we get for depending on Tom Hildreth. I told Dad he ought to send a wagon of his own to The Dalles as soon as the snow went off, but he wouldn't do it.'

Brad cuffed back his hat. 'Jeanie, did Cory ever make a mistake?'

'He made a mistake when he didn't send a wagon out...' She stopped as if sensing something in Brad's tone she didn't like. 'What kind of a fool question is that?'

'It was a fool question, I guess,' Brad admitted. 'I'll lug your stuff in. Tom had everything but the tomatoes.'

He carried the supplies in, and put the team away. He had to see Cory, and it wouldn't be an altogether pleasant talk. For half an hour he cut wood, wondering just what he would say.

Jeanie put her head through the kitchen window. 'Your dinner's ready, Brad.'

He drove the axe into the chopping block and, picking up an armful of wood, carried it into the kitchen. Cory had hobbled in from the front room and sat at the table, smoking his pipe.

'Good trip, Brad?' he asked.

'Fair.' Brad poured water into the wash basin from a bucket and washed the dust off and combed his hair. 'Dollit and Bailey were at Hildreth's.'

Cory took his pipe out of his mouth, dark eyes pinned on Brad. He had been a big man, decisive of motion and speech, but he had thinned down until his cheek bones seemed about to burst through his skin. His face, which had been deeply tanned, had lost its color. But there was a greater change in him than the mark of poor health, and Brad knew that Jeanie worried about it. Two months of idleness had gone hard with Cory Steele, and it galled him to be dependent upon his neighbors, for he was a man who had never depended upon anyone but himself.

Brad sat down and began to eat.

Jeanie asked: 'Want a cup of coffee, Dad?'

'No, thanks.' Cory had let his pipe go out. He fired it, pulling hard for a moment before he said: 'You act like you heard something.'

'I did. We've got a swamp angel in the valley.'

Cory emitted a sulphurous exclamation, and Brad went on to tell him what Dollit had said, adding: 'He asked a good question. Where does that leave us?'

'It don't change anything,' Cory said sharply. 'Dollit's lying.'

'Why would he lie?'

Cory shrugged his shoulders. 'Dunno, but I

don't trust Whang Dollit no more than you do. I always did figure he was more than just a man on the dodge. From the first day he hit this valley, he started his talk about how we couldn't last. Now he comes up with this.'

'You think there ain't no Riley Rand?'

'That I wouldn't know, but if there is, I'll bet my bottom dollar he ain't bought the valley from the state of Oregon.'

Brad finished his stewed prunes. Pushing back his chair, he said: 'You've got enough wood to last a few days, Jeanie.'

'Thanks,' Jeanie said. 'I don't know how we could have got along without you. Nick will be out Sunday. He can chop enough to run all week. You can't go on neglecting your own work like this.'

Brad had forgotten about young Bailey. He turned to Cory. 'Hildreth's worrying about Nick's drinking. He figures you can help him. Give him a job. Invite him out for a meal. Or something.'

'I'll do something. I'll break his danged neck. That'll stop his drinking.' Cory pulled himself upright and, balancing on his good leg, reached for his crutches that were leaning against the wall. 'Come in here, Brad. I've got talk to make.'

Cory hobbled into the front room, and dropped down on the leather couch where he spent most of his time. Brad hesitated, thinking of a dozen things he had to do at home.

Then Jeanie gave him a shove, whispering: 'Go on, Brad. He's lonesome.'

'I get lonesome, too,' Brad said.

Jeanie threw back her head and laughed. 'If you come over some evening when there's a full moon, I'll take care of that.'

'There's a dance Saturday night…,' Brad began.

She put a hand on his arm, her face showing genuine regret. 'I'm sorry, Brad. I'd be glad to go with you, but Nick's already asked me.'

Without another word Brad wheeled from her and stalked into the other room. Cory was filling his pipe, scowling. He motioned for Brad to sit down. Then he asked: 'What was the idea of telling me to help Nick?'

'Hildreth asked me to.'

'Tom's a fool. I don't figure Nick Bailey is worth saving, and I'm damned sure I don't want him hanging around here. I'll shoot him between the eyes before I'll let him marry Jeanie. He wasn't any good when we lived in the Willamette Valley, and now that he's running around with Dollit, he's worse than no good.'

'That what you wanted to say?'

'No. I'm gonna say something else first.' He held his pipe in his hand, dark eyes studying Brad a minute. Then he said in a low tone: 'I got the notion from a few things you've said that you were going to ask Jeanie to marry you.'

Brad rose. 'I can't. Not till I get ahead a little.'

'Sit down,' Cory said. 'Maybe I'm talking out of turn, Brad. But if you love Jeanie, you'll ask her to marry you. If you don't, why, just forget everything I've said.'

Brad sat down again, and leaned forward.

'I've loved Jeanie from the first time I saw her, and I'll go on loving her as long as I live, but everything I've got except my horse and saddle I'm in debt to you for. A man's got to have some pride if he's worth a damn. That's why I've held back. I wanted to get ahead a little.'

'And waste the best years of your life because of your pride?' Cory shook his head. 'You're wrong, Brad.' He shifted his weight, gritting his teeth against the pain. 'I ain't fooling myself, boy. This leg ain't getting no better. Maybe I'll never sit a saddle again. I dunno. I know one thing, though. You'd take care of my Jeanie if something happens to me, and Bailey wouldn't.'

Brad held his silence then, knowing he had said all he could say. He had been through this in his own mind many times. It wasn't entirely his pride that had held him back. Jeanie was nineteen, but Brad felt she would need another year before she would be ready to settle down. And then, too, his own prospects would be better at the end of the year.

'I'm sorry I said all of that,' Cory said finally. 'Just busted out of me. When it comes to marrying, a man has to decide for himself. What I wanted to talk about was something else.'

Cory took his pipe out of his mouth and looked down at it. 'Like I said, Brad, I ain't fooling myself. I can't get to a doctor, so I'll keep on being a cripple, or I'll get well according to what old Mother Nature says. Either way, I ain't much use to the folks I brought here. They need someone to do their fighting for 'em. The land we've settled ain't really swampland, and Riley Rand or nobody else is taking our places away from us. We'll fight...'

'Wilder,' a man called from outside, 'I told you to stay away from my girl!'

Brad rose and checked his gun, giving Cory a thin grin. 'Sounds like Nick Bailey. I guess he's a little proddy.'

Brad went out through the front door, and circled the house. Nick Bailey was sitting his saddle just beyond the chip pile, his hat cuffed at the back of his head, his thin face dark with the rage that gripped him. Jeanie stood looking up at him. She was talking in a tone so low that Brad could not hear what she was saying.

Brad stopped at the corner of the house. He said evenly: 'What's biting you, Nick?'

Jeanie whirled. 'Go back and stay with Dad. Nick wanted to see me.'

'That's funny. Sounded like he yelled at me.'

'No, he doesn't want to see you!' Jeanie cried in a ragged voice. 'Go on back.'

But Brad stood motionless, meeting Bailey's cold direct stare.

'Whang kept telling me how it was, Wilder,' Bailey said. 'I should have believed him all the time.'

'Just how did Whang say it was?' Brad asked coolly.

'He said you kept coming over here to help Cory out, but all you wanted to do was see Jeanie. He said you was just using Cory's trouble as an excuse.'

'It's a good excuse,' Brad said. 'A lot to be done around here that Jeanie can't do, but I ain't seen you were doing much of it. I've been figuring you were a mite lazy, Nick. Otherwise you could use the same excuse.'

'Brad, go back into the house,' Jeanie begged. 'This won't help any of us.'

Brad shook his head. 'Nick wanted to see me, Jeanie. I aim to give him so much chance to see me that he'll get a stomach full.'

'I got that already!' Bailey shouted. 'I'm sick of the sight of you. It's a purty danged poor excuse of a man that'll steal another man's girl. Jeanie and me was engaged when we left the Willamette Valley. Now I ain't sure how I stand with her since you horned in.'

'How about it, Jeanie?' Brad asked. 'You engaged to Bailey?'

She backed away, biting her lower lip, her face pale. 'He never gave me a ring. It was just kind of an understanding.' She whirled to face Bailey. 'You aren't being fair, talking this way, Nick. You couldn't expect a girl to marry you, the way you've acted since you got here.'

'You sound like your dad,' Bailey said bitterly. 'Before I left Getalong, Whang said I was a fool to let you kick me around like this. He said the only thing to do was to lick hell out of Wilder, and that's what I'm going to do.'

Bailey swung out of his saddle, unbuckled his gun, and tossed it on the ground beside the chopping block. Jeanie ran to him and gripped his arms.

'This won't settle anything, Nick. Get back on your horse. I'll see you at the dance Saturday night, and if you...'

'Take off your gun belt, Wilder,' Bailey said in a metal-thin voice. 'When I get done with you, you won't be in no shape to kiss my girl.'

Brad unbuckled his gun belt, and dropped it. Before it touched the ground, Bailey had pushed Jeanie roughly aside and came at Brad in a wild, senseless rush, both arms swinging. Brad stepped aside and threw a right that knocked Bailey flat.

Nick Bailey was a crazy man. He bounced

back up, wasting breath in a string of oaths. He was swinging from his knees and making no effort to defend himself, and for the second time Brad let go with a right. Bailey spilled out full-length on the ground and then sat up, shaking his head, blood running down his chin from a cut lip.

'If you've had enough,' Brad said, 'get on your horse and drift.'

Bailey said nothing. He got to his feet more slowly this time and moved in cautiously, his guard up. Brad stepped back, but Bailey caught him by the leg and brought him to the ground.

Brad went down hard, the fall knocking the wind out of him, and Bailey fell on him. They went over, Bailey underneath, and over again, Bailey using his knees and elbows. Brad heaved over, clubbed Bailey on the side of the head, and broke free. He got to his feet and stood there, waiting.

Bailey raised himself on one elbow and stared at Brad, hate in his eyes, blood drooling down his chin. He lay close to the chopping block, and now he rolled over in a sudden swift motion and grabbed for his gun belt. Brad was caught flat-footed, his own gun belt twenty feet behind him, but Brad took the chance of going for his gun, wheeling and lunging toward it. He heard Jeanie scream: 'Don't do it, Nick, don't do it!' Then Brad fell flat on his stomach, clawing desperately for his gun and knowing that time had run out for him. But the gun that sounded was not Bailey's .44. It was a rifle cracking from the kitchen door.

'Drop it,' Cory yelled. 'Drop it, or by gad my next slug is going into your brisket instead of the chopping block.'

Brad had his gun clear by then and was scrambling to his feet. Jeanie stood with both hands at her throat.

'I said drop it,' Cory repeated. 'I ain't saying it another time.'

Bailey let go of his gun. He came to his feet, still watching Cory. Without a word he moved past Brad, lurching drunkenly. He reached his horse and stood there a moment, gripping the horn, before he pulled himself into leather.

Brad walked toward him. He said: 'I've got nothing against you, Nick. Let's forget it.'

'I'll forget it when you're dead,' Bailey said thickly.

'Use your noggin,' Brad pressed. 'Go back to your folks and help 'em out. You haven't done a day's work since you started riding with Whang Dollit. That won't get you anywhere, and you know it.'

'It'll make me a sight more money than chasing after a few cows.'

Jeanie came up with his hat and handed it to him. She said in a low, tight voice: 'You tried to kill him, Nick. What's got into you?'

Bailey took the hat, and put it on. 'I will kill him,' he said. He gave Cory a wicked look, then reined around, and rode away.

'You can't make no mistake now, Jeanie!' Cory shouted. 'You've got Bailey's size. You got Brad's, too. You...' Then he lost his grip on the doorjamb and fell forward into the yard, face down.

Jeanie screamed and ran to him, Brad a step behind her. She knelt beside her father; she felt of his face, and took one of his thin hands in hers. She began to cry then and, looking up at Brad, asked: 'Is he dead?'

'Fainted, I reckon,' Brad said. He lifted Cory, carried him through the kitchen to the front room, and laid him on the couch, surprised at how light he was. He felt of Cory's pulse, and stood up. 'He's all right, Jeanie. He just hasn't got much strength any more.'

She sat down on a chair, her shoulders slack, her face very pale. She whispered: 'He was right about Nick, Brad. I've just been bull-headed.'

'I was wrong myself,' Brad said. 'I didn't figure he'd make a try for his gun.'

'What's happened to Nick?' she asked.

'I don't know,' Brad answered. 'I've been wondering what he meant when he said he'd make more money riding with Dollit than he would chasing after cows.'

Her hands fisted in her lap, clenched so tightly that her knuckles were white. 'I haven't been a very good daughter, Brad. I've wanted my own way. That's all. I haven't liked Nick for a long time.'

Turning, Brad left the room, and walked through the kitchen and on to the chip pile. He picked up Bailey's gun and belt, and jammed the .44 into the holster.

Cory was conscious when Brad came back into the house. When he saw Brad, he said: 'It's a great thing to be as useless as I am.'

Brad laid the gun on the table. 'Then I guess I ain't worth much. You just saved my life, you know.'

'You know I didn't mean that. Fainting was what I meant, flopping out there like a nervous woman looking at a spoonful of blood.'

'I'm gonna find this Riley Rand, if he's in the valley,' Brad said. 'I've got to see if any cows got bogged down first, then I'll take a sashay south to the rim and see if he's there like Dollit said.'

Cory gave him a straight look, his eyes very dark and bright against the pale gray of his face. 'What are you thinking, Brad?'

'Maybe what you were thinking a while ago. I reckon I'm just a little slower in the head than you are. Seems kind of funny, Dollit being right about a cowman coming here to the valley and Bailey saying he'd make money riding with Dollit. Looks like they're all playing the same tune.'

'Yeah, we're thinking the same thing. I figure there's a hook-up between 'em, all right, but they won't steal our homes, Brad. We'll fight 'em to hell and back.'

'Keep a gun handy,' Brad said. 'Jeanie, you'd best stick pretty close to home.'

'Why?' she asked.

'Because Cory's our brains. If he was dead, the settlers would scatter like a band of bleating sheep.'

She jumped up, her head back. 'Brad, you don't think Nick came out here to kill Dad? I thought...'

'I don't know,' Brad cut in. 'I just don't know, but things don't smell good.'

'I ain't sure about how smart you are, looking for this Rand *hombre*,' Cory said. 'Better get a few of the boys together before you start out.'

'I'll see,' Brad said, and turned to the door.

'Brad,' Cory said.

Brad stopped, and swung back. Cory was breathing hard, the corners of his mouth working a little as if he were under a great emotional strain.

'What is it?' Brad asked.

'This will be a fine valley in a few years, if we're let alone,' Cory said, 'but it's like you say. If I was dead, everybody'd run like sheep.' Cory wiped a hand across his forehead and brought it away damp with sweat. 'What I'm trying to say is that I feel like my sand's run out. It's gonna be up to you.'

'Me?' Brad stared at him, shocked. 'Why, I've just been a fiddlefoot as long as I can remember. Nobody can take your place, Cory. I couldn't, anyhow.'

Cory smiled. 'You could if you believed in something strong enough.'

Brad gestured wearily. 'Sure, I believe, but...'

'No buts.' Cory lifted a thin hand. 'Listen to me, boy. Listen close. I gambled on you right from the start, and I wasn't wrong. There isn't another fellow in the valley who can handle a gun like you can. You've got backbone, and you've got integrity. That's the big thing. If you've got that and enough faith, why … you can do anything.'

'You'd better get some sleep,' Brad said. 'I think you're out of your head.' He dropped the three silver dollars on the table that Hildreth had given him. 'There's your change. Almost forgot about it.'

He left the room, not looking at Jeanie. He saddled his buckskin that he had left in the corral and, mounting, rode around a shallow corner of the lake toward his cabin. He could not get Cory's words out of his mind. The trouble was Cory didn't know the whole truth. Brad had come along because Jeanie was coming. He had never told either Cory or Jeanie that, but he knew now he would have to tell Jeanie. He could wait no longer.

Brad looked southward to the frowning

rimrock, looked at the desert sweep of the land, tilting upward away from the lake, and he wondered what went into the making of a man like Cory Steele, what had given him his great faith, what made people look to him for leadership. Then something tightened inside Brad Wilder and brought an uneasiness to him. Today, without actually putting it into words, Cory had tried to tell him that he had a feeling he would not live to see done the things he had dreamed of doing.

Brad stopped at his cabin long enough to get into his 'muddling clothes'. He picked up a shovel that leaned against the wall beside the door, and stepped back into the saddle. Just west of his cabin lay a stretch of mud flat that was a deathtrap for cows. Even from here he could see that one was bogged down.

Something had to be done about the mud flat. A fence would have to be built, or the flat drained. There was no wire in the valley, and it was a long way to the Blue Mountains to get poles.

It was well along in the tag end of the afternoon now, with the sun dipping down toward the western rimrock, and a chill wind had come up that stirred the water of the lake into small chopping whitecaps. Brad dismounted and set to work digging the cow out.

By the time the job was done, Brad was cold and tired, his temper was whetted to a fine edge, and he looked like a mud man.

Brad did not see the three riders coming across the grass until one of them raised a hand, calling out: 'You Brad Wilder?'

The one who had called would be Riley Rand, Brad judged. Brad said – 'I'm Wilder.' – and waited, wondering about this. It seemed strange that a newcomer like Rand would know his name. Then he saw that one was a woman, the other a young man in his middle twenties, medium tall and slender.

They pulled up twenty feet away, Rand saying: 'Looks like you had a little fun.'

'In my book it ain't fun,' Brad said shortly, thinking he must be a sight, plastered with drying muck as he was.

'I'm Riley Rand,' the man said as if expecting his name to mean something.

He was a big man, this Rand, big and impressive-looking with a square jaw and bold blue eyes that were as frosty as two pieces of ice. He had long muscular arms and big hands, and there was about him the confident air of a man who would push and crowd and shove until anything and everybody who blocked his path had been moved aside.

'I've heard of you,' Brad said.

'My sister, Gail.'

Rand motioned to the woman who sat her side-saddle with cool grace. She was about twenty-five, Brad guessed, with blue eyes and hair as yellow as ripe bunchgrass. She gave an impression of tallness and had much the same air of complete self-confidence that her brother had. Irritation stirred in Brad as he touched his hat brim. She was giving him a look of sharp appraisal as if wondering just what sort of man was under all the mud.

Rand indicated the man to his left. 'Wilder, meet Smoke Kinnear. You've probably heard of him.'

Masking his face against the shock of surprise, Brad said: 'Howdy, Kinnear. Ain't you off your reservation a little?'

'A little,' Kinnear said.

Brad had heard of the man all right. Anyone who had spent some time in the Southwest would have heard of Smoke Kinnear. He carried two .44s, butts forward, the holsters low and tied down in the manner favored by professionals. He had a thin face with a saber-sharp nose and pale blue eyes that were insolently defiant.

Brad had expected Rand to shout loudly that he owned the valley and was giving everybody so many days to clear out. But Rand did nothing of the kind. He fired his cigar, glancing at the few cows grazing to his right.

'How many head of cattle in the valley, Wilder?' he asked then, his tone friendly.

''Bout a thousand.'

'How many people?'

'Twenty families and a few single men.'

Rand scratched his wide chin, looking at the lake and frowning. 'They tell me that when this swampland is drained and the tules cleaned out, you have wonderful grass land. Sort of sub-irrigated, I suppose.'

'I've heard that,' Brad said carefully, wondering what Rand was getting at.

'Just what sort of claim do these settlers have to their land, Wilder?' Rand asked.

'Squatters' rights.'

'I see,' Rand said. 'Kind of risky, ain't it, settling here without knowing they'll ever be able to file on their places?'

'Maybe.'

Rand grinned. 'Well, we're just taking a ride to see what the valley looks like.' He jabbed a forefinger at a cabin a quarter of a mile to the west. 'Who lives there?'

'Al Benton and his wife and three kids.'

Rand jerked his head at the others. 'Let's ride. We'll see you again, Wilder.'

They turned their horses westward and rode away. Brad watched them for a minute, still puzzled, and then swung his buckskin toward his cabin. Dollit, he supposed, had told them his name. The talk, to Brad's way of thinking, made less than sense. Rand didn't look much like a schemer. Why hadn't he just come out and said he owned the valley and to get off his land?

Brad put his horse away, and went into the cabin, still wondering about Rand. He was washing up when he heard a horse. It was Rand's sister Gail.

Brad stepped to the door. He said: 'Howdy, miss.'

She came in, giving him that sharp look of appraisal again. She smiled then. It was as if a shade had been lifted from her face. She seemed very friendly, the calculating sharpness gone from her eyes. 'I guess you didn't expect me to come calling.' She gave a quick glance around the room that was bare of everything except the sheer necessities for living, and brought her eyes up to him again. 'Opening up a new country is a grim life for a while, isn't it?'

'We were getting along,' he said, irritation

growing in him.

'You need a woman, Mister Wilder. I never could see any reason for a man living alone. But then I hear you have your loop on a girl.'

'You've heard a lot in the time you've been here,' he said hotly. 'If you want to give advice, try handing some out to your brother.'

Her lips tightened. 'I'm sorry, Mr Wilder. I didn't come here to give you advice. Not this kind, and, as for my brother, he doesn't take advice. I've tried.' She smiled again, apologetically. 'Believe me, I came here for two reasons, both friendly. One was to tell you to watch out for Smoke Kinnear.'

'If you think I spook that easy...'

She raised a hand. 'Now, Mister Wilder, you're sizing me up wrong. I told you I came for friendly reasons. You strike me as being a man who can take care of himself in almost any situation, but, you see, Kinnear isn't a man. He's a machine, a killing machine.'

She was frankly pleading with him now, and the anger went out of him. He said: 'All right. I'm warned. I'll watch out for him.'

'That's better. You see, my brother and I don't agree on ways and means. The trouble with Riley is that he believes anything is all right, if it works.' She hesitated, and then shook her head. 'Maybe I'm wasting my time and yours, too, but the real reason I came was to ask you to have supper with us tonight.'

It was the most surprising thing she could have said. He hesitated, wondering if this was a trap.

'I'd like to,' he said, 'but...'

'I know what you're thinking. We're enemies by virtue of our position, but re-member, Mister Wilder, that there are several grades of enemies. You said there were twenty families here in the valley. What happens in the next few days will determine whether the women and children of these families are left without husbands and fathers.'

So that was it! Again anger crowded him. He shouted: 'If you think we'll bluff...!'

'You can stop right there. Riley is a hard man. He wouldn't have Smoke Kinnear with him if he wasn't. The point is I'm not as willing to shed blood as Riley is. A friendly talk won't hurt, and it might help. Tomorrow will be too late.'

Again he had the feeling she was pleading with him. He sensed an earnestness about her that seemed sincere.

'All right. I'll be along as soon as I shave,' he said.

'Thank you. Our camp is directly south of here.'

Half an hour later Brad was riding south, the sun barely showing above the western rimrock. By the time he reached the Rand camp, the valley lay shrouded under purple dusk. There were two wagons, he saw, and a tent that was possibly Gail's. A Chinese cook was bending over the Dutch ovens as Brad dismounted.

Riley Rand drifted up, saying: 'Glad you could come.'

'Friendly of your sister to ask me,' Brad said.

Rand laughed softly. 'It was her idea. We're

a lot alike, Gail and me, when it comes to going after what we want, but we're different when it comes to method. Oh, Wilder, meet George McCloud.'

Another man had come up, a short, heavyset young man who was a little too paunchy for his years. He was wearing a brown broadcloth suit and a black derby, and, when he held out his hand, Brad found that it was soft and a little moist.

'Glad to know you, Wilder,' McCloud said, his voice definitely that of an Easterner.

'Howdy,' Brad said.

Kinnear sat hunkered by the fire, smoking. He ignored Brad's presence completely. Gail came out of the tent, calling: 'Just in time, Mister Wilder! I've been eating like a horse ever since we left Nevada. There's something about your air up here that does things to my appetite.'

'Here, here,' McCloud said. 'He doesn't own the air, you know. That's just taking in too much.'

'He doesn't own the land, either, George,'

Rand said. 'We own it. Let's make that clear. Squatters' rights don't hold against a patent.'

'No more of that,' Gail said sharply. 'We'll talk business after supper.'

'A good idea,' McCloud said heartily. 'I don't want my appetite spoiled. That's the trouble with my brother. You've heard of him, Wilder, John McCloud, the railroad man.'

'Yes, reckon I have,' Brad agreed.

'Well, he's always talking business, morning, noon, and night. That's why I'm here. Had to get away from it. I've got all the money I want. I learned a long time ago that the simple life is the best. This wilderness is paradise. Living in the open, breathing that air Gail was...'

'Let's eat, George,' Gail said impatiently. 'When you get to talking, you just about starve me to death.'

'Oh, I'm sorry, my dear,' McCloud said apologetically. 'I'm awfully sorry.'

But McCloud kept up his talk. Gail was plainly bored, and Brad seemed to be only half listening. Kinnear had taken his plate and tin cup and drifted away.

Time ribboned out into minutes and piled up into half an hour. The last trace of the sunset left the sky. Thunder boomed from somewhere off to the south. Rand tossed some pieces of juniper on the fire and watched the blaze. 'I hear a man named Cory Steele is the big gun among the settlers, and he's laid up. That right?' Rand said, his eyes on the fire.

'That's right.'

'I also hear that he's got a pile of gold hidden in his cabin. Dangerous, it seems to me, in a country like this.'

'Just a rumor,' Brad said. 'How'd you hear it?'

'Oh, a man picks up things like that,' Rand answered.

'Dollit's tale, I suppose,' Brad said, and, picking up his plate and cup, carried them to the wreck pan. 'Don't believe all his yarns, Rand.'

'Dollit?' Rand said as if he couldn't place the name. 'Oh, yes, he was the settler who rode in last night to see who we were. Acted like he owned the country.'

Brad returned to stand with the fire between him and Rand. Kinnear had drifted back. He stood spread-legged, hands at his sides, his barren face expressionless, pale eyes on Brad. McCloud had moved away toward one of the wagons, and suddenly it struck Brad that Gail was not in sight.

'Might as well get down to cases,' Rand said easily. 'You've probably guessed why we asked you here. If you've seen Dollit, he may have told you that I have bought this valley from the state, not knowing that any settlers were here. Now I'm faced with a problem. I want them out of the country before my herd gets here.'

'Why don't you talk to Cory Steele?' Brad asked.

'Two reasons. He's laid up, so I'm counting him out. Second reason is that I hear he's a fanatic, one of these fellows who won't budge for hell or high water. That's why I'm hoping I can do business with you.' He lifted a cigar from his pocket and bit off the end, bold eyes bright in the firelight. 'A bunch of settlers always has someone who calls the turn. It's been Steele, but with him on his back it'll be you.'

'You're wrong on that,' Brad said.

'I don't think so. I can use a man of your caliber in my organization. I pay a good man well, as Smoke can tell you. How about it, Wilder?'

Brad saw it then. He was elected to be an example. He'd be bought, or he'd die. A rage boiled up in him, a cold compelling rage. He had believed Gail Rand and he'd been sucked into a trap. They were alike, Gail and Riley Rand, but because Gail was a woman, she had brought the invitation. The talk about warning him against Smoke Kinnear had been part of the bait, but she had been right about one thing. Kinnear was a killing machine.

Brad was good with a gun, but he stood little chance against Kinnear. Then Brad was remembering some of the things Cory Steele had said, and he knew what Cory would say if he were here. It was a cheap way to clear the valley, a cheap dirty way characteristic of Riley Rand. With Cory laid up and Brad out of the way, there would be no one else to make a stand. Rimrock O'Shay, the Widow Bain, Al Benton, Tom Hildreth. He could name them all. They had followed Cory here, and, without him, they'd go.

So Brad Wilder made his decision. George McCloud and Riley Rand were watching him, waiting. No sound but the crackling of the juniper. A flame leaped up, touching Kinnear's barren face.

'Crawl back under a rock, Rand,' Brad said, spacing each word so that it was a slap in Rand's face. 'You can go to blazes.'

Then Rand moved away, leaving Kinnear and Brad facing each other across the fire.

Chapter Two

For a moment there was no sound but the crackling of the fire and McCloud's heavy breathing. Smoke Kinnear took a sadistic pleasure in watching Brad look at the face of death. But Kinnear didn't draw.

Gail's voice cut across the space between them: 'You make a move for your guns, Smoke, and I'll blow your head off.'

'Get back into your tent!' Rand bellowed. 'Of all the fool things to do…'

'Shut up,' Gail said. 'You always claim a man can do anything with dollars and guns. If Smoke makes a fast move, I'll show you what a woman can do with buckshot.'

'My dear girl…,' McCloud began.

'You shut up, too, George!' Gail cried. 'I'm running this show till Wilder is out of camp.'

'Then I'll be moseying,' Brad said. 'I wasn't

counting on this.'

Kinnear gave him a small grin. 'Me, neither, Wilder. When Rand hired me, he didn't say he had a hellcat of a sister.'

'I didn't know it myself,' Rand said.

'Get on your horse, Wilder,' Gail said. 'I'm apologizing for the Rand style of hospitality. It won't happen again.'

'You ain't stopped nothing, miss,' Kinnear breathed.

'I don't care about stopping anything. If you and Wilder want to swap lead, it's your business, but it wasn't part of the deal Riley agreed to, and I'll see he keeps his word if I have to convince him with buckshot.'

Brad backed toward his horse, and stepped up. 'You think maybe I'm a mite faster'n your hired man, Miss Rand?'

'No, but when I invite anyone to eat with us, I don't propose to see him murdered.'

'She's right,' Rand conceded, 'but I hold a pat hand, Wilder. You and your neighbors can sit tight and make me force you off my grass, or you can go peacefully and save trouble for all of us. Which will it be?'

'I ain't speaking for my neighbors,' Brad said, 'but I will speak for me and Cory Steele. We'll fight you to hell and back. If you ever get our places, you'll have the chore of buying us on 'em. Don't you forget that.'

'We could attend to that chore.' Rand scratched his head as if puzzled. 'I don't savvy you, Wilder. You're too smart to think the Land Office'll recognize squatters' rights to land that has been bought from the state.'

'That's right,' Brad agreed, 'but I think you're a liar and a thief.'

'Get out of camp, Wilder!' Gail called. 'Don't push your luck too far.'

Rand's big body stiffened, and his face flamed with fury.

Brad laughed softly. 'The truth don't sound good to you, does it, Rand? All right, miss, I'll be glad to ride out of here.'

Reining around, Brad headed north, putting his buckskin into a run. When the campfire had become a small red eye in the night, he pulled down to a walk. Sweat broke out on his body as relief rushed through him. He had never wiggled out of a tighter spot than this. He had no illusions about how his gun speed compared with Kinnear's. It had been sheer pride that had made him face Kinnear across the campfire.

Brad was able to smile now that the threat of death had passed. He was thankful to be alive. He was even glad it had happened, for now he understood the Rands. Perhaps he had been foolish to slap Riley with such jarring insults, but it didn't make any difference. He had pledged himself to hang and rattle. His big job would be to persuade the settlers to fight, but he had a feeling that Cory was the only one who could do it.

While he was putting his horse in the corral, it occurred to him he was following Cory's hunch that Rand had not bought the valley. If Cory was wrong, there was no use in fighting. Rand had been right in saying the Land Office would not recognize squatters' rights, if the land had actually been sold. Cory would know that, too, so he must have based his belief on something more solid than a hunch.

Lightning was playing over the sky now, thunder booming steadily overhead. Rain would come soon. Brad barred the door, and went to bed. For a time he lay awake, wondering what Rand's next move would be. Whatever it might be, it would come soon. Then his mind turned to the Easterner. George McCloud seemed entirely out of place with the Rands and Kinnear. He was too soft for this country.

When Brad woke, the sky was cloudless. There was no wind, and the lake was as placid as a great tule-lined mirror. Brad built a fire, then went outside and watered and fed his buckskin. He returned to the cabin and cooked breakfast, watching the valley to the south, for he expected to see Kinnear and Rand ride up.

When he finished eating, he thought of borrowing Cory's team and going after a load of wood. He gave it up at once, for it was a long trip, and this was no time to be gone from the valley.

This was the sort of situation he hated, waiting and worrying and trying to outguess Riley Rand. Brad rolled a smoke, eyes swinging to the south. Nothing was visible except a few cows. He remembered that Al Benton wanted to butcher a shoat. He'd ride over and see if Benton wanted to do the job today. Benton was typical of the settlers, a hard worker who, if let alone, would someday make a home here for his family. While they were butchering, he'd find out if Benton wanted that home enough to fight for it.

Brad saddled his buckskin and stood beside the horse, staring westward. Whang Dollit and Nick Bailey were riding toward him. They had come, he guessed, from Benton's, and he wondered if their visit had anything to do with Rand. He made a quick check of his gun, and eased it back into leather.

'Hey, Wilder!' Dollit called, and motioned to him.

Brad watched the two men ride in. He said

– 'Howdy, Whang.' – keeping his eyes on Bailey as they reined up. Bailey's face showed the marks of Brad's fists but otherwise was a mask of surly indifference.

'We're doing a chore for Riley Rand and ourselves,' Dollit said. 'Remember what I said about us having a little nuisance value?'

'Yeah, I remember. Are you Rand's chore boy?'

Anger stained Dollit's dark-jowled face. He said sharply: 'We ain't hunting trouble, mister, but we ain't against handling it if it bobs up.'

'I ain't been hunting it, neither, but it sure as hell has been hunting me.'

Dollit laughed as if this was extremely funny. 'I heard about that. From the look of Nick's mug, I guess you handled that piece of trouble.'

'Shut up,' Bailey said. 'We ain't here on that account.'

Dollit shrugged. 'Why, I ain't one to horn into another man's ruckus.' He nodded at Brad. 'Now just get this notion that I'm running Rand's errands out of your noggin, Wilder. I'm the kind of hairpin who looks out for number one.'

'You gonna tell him?' Bailey demanded.

'Yeah. Rand wants to see the settlers in Getalong this afternoon, Wilder. About three. You be there.'

'Why?'

'No good reason, maybe,' Dollit said smugly, 'but was I you, I'd be there. We ain't in no shape to buck Rand, so I say we'd best cash in on our nuisance value if we can.'

'I'm bucking him,' Brad said flatly.

Dollit grinned as if pleased. 'That's your business, friend. I've wanted to see you whittled down ever since I hit the valley. Riley Rand is just the gent who can do it.'

'I'm here, and you're here,' Brad said. 'Why wait for Rand?'

Dollit shook his head. 'I'm willing to let Rand do the whittling. I want to get what I can, and then ride out of here. Come on, Nick.'

'Wait a minute,' Brad said. 'Nick, your folks

have got a claim. Are they gonna pull out?'

'Dunno,' Bailey said, and rode off.

Dollit was in the best humor Brad had ever seen him. Dollit thought, grinning: *They'll pull out all right, but I'm hoping you don't. I'll laugh my head off when Rand nails your hide to your cabin door.* Still grinning, Dollit spurred his horse and caught up with Bailey.

For a long moment Brad stood still, squinting against the bright morning sunlight. This, then, was Rand's move. He'd buy the settlers off if he could. Gail had said he believed a man could do anything with dollars and guns. He'd offer the dollars and threaten with guns, and the chances were good that the combination would work.

Brad remembered Gail had said yesterday that tomorrow would be too late. But tomorrow was today, and it still might not be too late. Paying the settlers something for their rights had probably been Gail's idea. Apparently her brother had thought that with Cory Steele laid up and Brad Wilder dead, guns would do the job without the dollars, but Gail must have had her way.

Mounting, Brad rode eastward, wondering what Cory would say. Rand would not make a big offer. Even if he did, no amount could pay the settlers for the labor and dreams that would be wasted. Brad knew how it was, for he was much like the others. Only Cory Steele and Tom Hildreth had money. The rest had their bare hands, perhaps a team and wagon and a few tools.

A generation before they could have found almost unlimited free and good land. Now most of those places were gone, but the hunger to own their land was as great as it had been with their predecessors. Then, if a man saw a good piece of land he liked, he could claim it and make a home if he had the courage to hold it. That day was gone. It was Blue Lake Valley or nothing, and it would be nothing if Riley Rand had his way.

When Brad came within sight of Cory's place, he saw that Dollit and Bailey had gone on. Quick relief washed through him for he did not want to tangle with Bailey again. The next time would be final, and he didn't want Jeanie to see it.

Jeanie came out of the house as Brad stepped down and tied. She said nothing until he turned to face her, and he saw that her dark eyes were troubled.

'Dollit and Nick were just here,' Jeanie said. 'They said there was a meeting with this Rand. What's he up to, Brad?'

'I ain't sure,' Brad said. 'How's Cory?'

'Poorly. He didn't sleep much last night.'

Brad followed her into the house, the slim hope that Cory would be able to go to the meeting dying in him. Cory was stretched out on the leather couch, a pillow under his head. He raised a thin hand in greeting, and his voice was clear and natural when he said: 'I had a notion you'd be along, Brad. I didn't get my talking all done yesterday, but I will this morning. Sit down.'

'I've got some talking to do myself. Want to hear my yarn first?'

Cory nodded, and began filling his pipe. 'Go ahead.'

Brad told him what had happened at the Rand camp, Cory smoking without comment. Jeanie stood by the kitchen door, listening.

When Brad finished, Cory said: 'Nothing's changed.'

'A lot is changed,' Brad said irritably. 'Rand's got a trail herd coming. If he turns his buckaroos loose on the valley, we're finished.'

'Then we'll do the job before his herd gets here,' Cory said coolly. 'Nothing's changed.' He motioned to Jeanie. 'Get dinner started.'

'It's too early.'

'No, it ain't. Brad's going to Getalong, and I figured you'd like to ride in with him.'

Jeanie disappeared into the kitchen.

Cory knocked out his pipe and motioned Brad closer. 'I'm gonna do my talking now. I ain't surprised about Rand's trying to run a sandy on us by claiming he's bought the valley. I've been trying to buy it myself.' Cory laughed when he saw Brad's surprise. 'I didn't tell anybody but Jeanie. I knew the valley had been declared swampland, but somebody's been blocking me in Salem. Must be Rand. If he gets us out of here, he'll move his herd in. Then all he's got to do is sit tight. Possession is nine points of the law.'

'Then you've been playing more'n a hunch.'

Cory filled his pipe, struck a match, and sucked the flame into the bowl. 'More'n a hunch, but on deals like this you can't be sure. Been a lot of criticism of the way the swampland has been handled. A few men get a big acreage, which same gives the state the sale price of the land, but it don't give many folks a home. That was my ace in the hole. I promised to settle the valley, and I've written to the Land Office telling 'em what I done. For three months I've been looking for a letter saying the deal had gone through, but so far not a word.' Cory shifted his weight, biting his lip against the pain that racked his gaunt body. He said: 'It's this damned leg that's stopped me. No use trying to go to the meeting. It's up to you.'

'I can't...'

'You can, and you will. What happened last night took all the doubts out of my mind.' He chewed on his pipe stem a moment, dark eyes studying Brad. 'You knew Kinnear could pull faster'n you could. Why did you make a pigeon out of yourself?'

'Pride, I reckon. If I'd caved, I'd never have been able to live with myself again.'

'It was more than that, Brad. Maybe you were thinking of Jeanie and the home you want to make for her, but I'm guessing it was mostly because you knew that with me knocked out and you pushing up the clods, Riley Rand would have every settler out of the valley in less than a week.'

Brad shrugged. 'Have it your way,' he muttered.

Cory laughed softly. 'I know how it is because there was a time when I was a lot like you. A good hand with a gun but not worth a damn. Just a fiddlefoot looking for a fighting job.' Cory drew a deep breath, his face bleak as memories rushed into his mind. 'I done a lot of things I ain't proud of. If you're honest, you'll admit you've done a few. That's right, ain't it?'

Brad rose, and walked to the door. 'Yeah, that's right.'

'I thought so. You or me could have been another Whang Dollit or Smoke Kinnear. You said the Rand woman called him a killing machine. That's a good name. Maybe it's what's down inside a man that makes the difference. Maybe it's other people that changes him. With me it was Jeanie's mother. With you maybe it's Jeanie.'

'Maybe,' Brad said from the doorway, his back to Cory.

'I'll never forget the first time I saw you,' Cory went on, 'riding that buckskin like you wasn't going nowhere and didn't give a damn. Toting a gun like you knew how to use it. You know what I thought when I saw you look at Jeanie?'

'No.'

'I was seeing myself twenty years earlier. Reckon I had the same kind of a look on my face the first time I seen Jeanie's mother. I said to myself here was a boy I had to take along. Maybe it was crazy, me not knowing anything about you, but I wasn't wrong. I had a feeling about you I can't put into words.

Brad came back to the couch. 'Why are you telling me this?'

'Why, I guess I want to prove to myself I was right about you.'

'I ain't sloping out if that's what you mean.'

Cory shook his head. 'It's more'n that, boy. You can't do much alone. If you can hold our bunch together, make 'em turn Rand down no matter how much he offers ... why, he's licked. As soon as we get news that the land's mine, Rand won't have a leg to stand on.'

'I can't talk to 'em,' Brad said.

'You'll know what to say when the time comes. Jeanie will be there to side you. Hildreth, too. He's sound. Rand'll be tough, if he can push folks, but I'll bet my bottom dollar he don't want a U.S. marshal in here.'

Jeanie came in from the kitchen. 'Dinner's

ready. Want to come to the table, Dad?'

Cory shook his head. 'Fetch it in here.'

She went out again.

Cory said: 'I told you yesterday I was a leader, but I wasn't when I was your age. I don't know when I learned how to get folks to do what I wanted 'em to but I did. I ain't even sure why.'

Jeanie brought Cory's tray in, and he sat up, pushing the pillow to his back. 'Tell 'em that I'll sell their land to 'em and take their notes and give 'em all the time they need.'

Jeanie laid the tray on Cory's lap. She said: 'We'd better eat.'

'I still don't savvy,' Brad said.

Cory laughed. 'I'll tell you what's the matter. It's the two months I've laid here staring at the ceiling. Nothing to do but think.' He waved toward the kitchen. 'Go get your dinner, Brad. When you get to town, you ask Hildreth about the mail.'

Brad followed Jeanie into the kitchen. She filled the coffee cups, saying softly: 'There's something he didn't tell you, Brad. He thinks he's going to die.'

'Well,' Brad said, 'I never heard of a man dying from a broken leg.'

He looked across the table at Jeanie, sensed she was thinking the same thing he was. Cory Steele wasn't worrying about dying from a broken leg.

Brad saddled Jeanie's horse while she changed her clothes. He waited in front of the cabin with the horses until she came out, her Stetson dangling down her back from the chin strap. She was wearing a brown riding skirt and a dark blouse; she moved toward him in the quick, graceful way that he had always liked. He gave her a hand up, and for a moment her hand remained in his as she looked down at him.

'Dad has his gun, Brad. He'll be all right.' She paused, biting her lower lip. 'He will be all right, won't he?'

'Sure,' he said, hiding the doubt he felt.

They talked little as they rode north. Brad inwardly resented the job Cory Steele had thrown into his lap but still knew he would do what he could. It was not likely there would be any powder burned today, for Riley Rand would be playing a benevolent rôle, saying he wanted to be fair, that he appreciated the work they had done, and would pay them something for their labor.

Brad tried to think of the right words to make the settlers see that Rand was a thief, wanting to force them off the grass so he could write to Salem and say he was the only one in the valley. His cattle were already grazing here, he'd say, and they'd keep on grazing whether he owned the land or not. The state could take his payment or turn it down.

If the settlers did not take Rand's offer, it would mean war. Rand would leave no doubt in their minds about what would happen. They might have a few days of grace before the herd reached the valley. That would be all. The words Brad needed would come to him. He could only hope that they would come when he needed them, as Cory had said they would.

It was a good day, filled with sunlight, and it struck Brad that there should never be trouble here. This valley had enough water and grass and land for everyone. Time! That was the one thing they didn't have, not with Riley Rand in the valley and with Smoke Kinnear to back any play he made, Kinnear, the killing machine. It boiled down to the age-old decision of fighting or crawling, or dying or living with the shame that comes with crawling. Brad and Cory knew it was better to die than live with that shame, but the others had not yet learned.

A sense of impending failure settled upon Brad. He glanced at Jeanie, wanting to tell her he loved her, to ask her to wait for him until he could give her the home he wanted his wife to have. Time! That was the answer to every problem here in the valley. But there was no time. He had to wait. If he died this day, or the next, or the day after that, it was better for her if she didn't know.

She smiled at him and asked: 'What are you thinking about, Brad?'

'Trouble,' he said.

Her smile left her lips. 'I know. Funny, isn't it, how we go along for a year without having anything go wrong? Then all of a sudden trouble piles up until you can't see over the top.'

'Yeah,' he said. 'Funny.'

They were opposite the Widow Bain's place, a tiny cabin too small for her and her five children. She had lost her husband the winter before. If there had been a doctor in the valley, Jim Bain might have been saved, but the closest doctor was on the other side of the Blue Mountains. So Jim's widow was left with the children, and only Tom Hildreth's generosity had kept them alive.

The widow was hitching up her wagon. She called out: 'I'll be along, Brad! Don't you let nothing happen till I get there.'

'I'll hold the lid on!' he shouted.

'Cory couldn't come?'

'No,' Jeanie called. 'He isn't well!'

'Too bad. We need him today.'

The widow's word burned Brad's mind

like a hot iron. *We need him today.*

A few minutes later old Rimrock O'Shay fell in with them, riding a plow horse that was so slow Brad and Jeanie had to pull their animals down to a snail's pace.

O'Shay asked: 'What's this all about?'

'Didn't Dollit tell you?' Brad asked.

'He said something about a cattleman claiming the valley, but, hell, Cory wouldn't have fetched us here unless the land was open for filing. I kept telling him we oughta hike out for Lakeview and file, but he said we didn't have time. Then he got laid up and couldn't go.'

'A paper claim wouldn't make no difference to a man like Riley Rand,' Brad said. 'The homestead law never has meant anything to cattlemen. There's only one thing that does.'

'You're talking about fighting,' O'Shay said bitterly. 'Well, you'll fight alone, Wilder. I've got a wife and a cabin full of kids.' His faded eyes were bleak as they stared across the valley. 'Sure too bad a man's foresight ain't as good as his hindsight. If I'd knowed Cory was gonna get bucked off a horse and laid up at a time like this, I'd have stayed in the Willamette Valley.'

They'll all think the same way, Brad thought. Cory could talk to them, make them believe that fighting and dying was better than crawling and living. A sense of impending failure shadowed Brad's thoughts. If Cory Steele were on his feet – but he wasn't, and no amount of wishful thinking could change that one hard fact.

They rode into Getalong a few minutes before three. The settlers were here, Brad saw at once, all but the Widow Bain, and she'd be along. Several groups were scattered between Hildreth's store and his house; talk rose, a low, worried hum. Dollit and Nick Bailey were standing in front of the saloon with Bailey's father. Dollit's voice rose above the hum. 'You boys can do as you damn' please, but me, I'm taking what I can get.'

Brad dismounted and gave a hand to Jeanie. Several people crowded around them, asking: 'How's Cory?' Jeanie's answer was always the same: 'He's poorly. He said he wished he could be here, but he couldn't.'

Brad tied his and Jeanie's horses. Old man Bailey drifted up, asking: 'What was the trouble between you and Nick?'

'Didn't Nick tell you?'

'No. He said you beat hell out of him.'

Brad told him what had happened, watching the old man's bitter eyes darken with anger, and he added: 'Nick would have blowed my head off if Cory hadn't horned in. You ain't got much cause to be proud of him since he started traveling with Dollit.'

'No,' Bailey said somberly. 'We should have stayed in the Willamette Valley. We was making a living there. Not much, but a living.' He spread his work-gnarled hands in a gesture of hopeless resignation. 'Nick's got a place beside mine, you know, but he don't work it. Now he's saying he'll take anything this Rand fellow will give him.'

'What about you?'

Bailey stared past Brad at the long dark

crest of the Blue Mountains. 'I reckon I'll quit, too. Nick's got some good in him, if I can get him away from Dollit. Maybe he'll go back to the Willamette Valley with me.'

Brad walked away, not wanting to hurt the old man, but it'd take a father, he thought, to see any good in Nick Bailey. Hildreth was in the store talking to Rand and Kinnear. Gail was not in sight. Hildreth stopped when he saw Brad come in. Rand and Kinnear turned, and for a moment Brad faced them, wondering if this was the time, but Kinnear's stony face told him nothing, and Rand hid his feelings behind a mask of friendliness.

'Howdy, neighbor,' Rand said. 'Still gonna hang tight?'

'You're damned right I am.' Brad nodded at Hildreth. 'Mail get in, Tom?'

'No, it ain't,' Hildreth answered. 'Three days overdue. I could understand if it was bad weather, but nothin's happened to hold him up. I can't figure it out.'

'Expecting something?' Rand asked.

'Cory was,' Brad said, turning away.

A moment later Hildreth left the store, Kinnear and Rand behind him. Hildreth called: 'All right, folks. It's three o'clock. Time to start.' He climbed the creaking stairs, Rand and Kinnear following. The others hesitated, then formed a line and moved up behind them.

Brad waited for Jeanie who was with the Widow Bain. They fell in behind the rest, and, when Brad was halfway up, he looked down and saw that Gail and Mrs Hildreth had just left the house. That was something else to wonder about. Gail had her place in this thing, and it occurred to Brad that she was more to be feared than her brother Riley. Women seldom understood what it meant to a man to fight. Mrs Hildreth was a tall pale woman who had hated this country from the first.

A table had been placed at the far end of the hall. Rand sat behind it, pen, ink, and paper in front of him. Kinnear lounged against the wall behind Rand, silent and watchful. Half a dozen benches had been arranged in front of the table. Most of the settlers sat down, but Brad remained standing behind Jeanie who sat beside the widow on the rear bench. Looking at the settlers' slumped shoulders, it seemed to Brad that they were beaten before Riley Rand opened his mouth.

Hildreth had been leaning over the table, talking to Rand. Now he turned ponderously, facing the crowd gravely. He said: 'Folks, this is a sad occasion. We've come a long ways to find a home, but looks like we picked the wrong spot.' He sucked in a wheezing breath. 'If Cory Steele were here, he'd be standing before you, but he's doing too poorly to be here, so I'm taking over long enough to introduce Riley Rand to you. I'll let him make his own spiel.'

Rand rose as Hildreth sat down. Rand unfolded a map and held it up. 'This is a sad occasion for me, too. As you can see on this official map, Blue Lake Valley has been declared swampland by the federal government and turned over to the state of Oregon. It was not open for settlement when you came here a year ago, and it isn't open now.' Rand laid the map on the table. 'Since Cory Steele is not here, I can't ask him the question that is in my mind and must be in yours. Why did he fetch you here and tell you to settle on land he must have known could not be filed on? Now whether he had some purpose of his own, or just didn't look into the situation, I don't know. Either way, it's rough on you and me, too.'

Fury rose in Brad. This was something he should have expected. Riley Rand was coolly setting out to break the settlers' trust in Cory at a time when he wasn't here to defend himself. Brad started around the bench, plenty of words in his mind now, but Jeanie caught him by his arm.

'Wait, Brad,' she whispered. 'Let's give him all the rope he needs.'

He hesitated, looking down at the girl's anxious face and thinking that Cory had foreseen this. He'd probably told Jeanie what to do. Brad nodded, and stepped back behind her.

'Now I'll tell you what I meant by saying this was rough on both of us,' Rand went on in a voice that was both worried and friendly. 'I have nothing against you folks. You trusted the wrong man, so the mistake wasn't yours. On the other hand, I bought this valley from the state, not knowing it had been settled. I came on ahead of my herd to see how the grass was and found you folks already here and your cattle eating my grass.'

'How come you could buy the valley when any fool can see that not much more'n a tenth of it is swampland?' Rimrock O'Shay demanded.

'I hadn't seen the land,' Rand answered easily. 'I bought it by looking at a map, and the map says it's swampland. Well, it's all right. When I reclaim the swamp, as I have to do according to the terms of the sale, I'll have good hay land. I don't mind saying, folks, that the valley suits me. In another ten years, you'll see the finest cattle ranch in Oregon right here in Blue Lake Valley.'

'I mean how could the state sell land that ain't swamp?' O'Shay persisted.

'The answer to that, my friend, is simple. The state needs money. Nobody in Salem cares whether it's swamp or sage flat as long as the government turns it over and some-one has money to pay for it.'

Rand paused, bold blue eyes sweeping the room, big hands, palms down, on the table. Even Brad found it hard to believe he was lying, for Riley Rand had the air of a man who could not be doubted and could not be stopped.

'So you see, folks, you have no legal claim to your homes,' Rand resumed. 'I could give you twenty-four hours to get out of the valley, but that wouldn't be fair. You do have a sort of moral claim, and, as I said, the mistake was not yours. So I'm willing to pay you for your improvements, providing you'll sign over whatever rights you think you have. Actually you don't have any because no Land Office will recognize squatters' rights in the face of a sale like this, but I want to get something

87

for my money.' Stooping, Rand lifted several small sacks to the top of the table, the soft *clink* of gold coming to Brad through the oppressive silence. 'I told you I wanted to be fair,' Rand assured them. 'I'll give you five hundred dollars apiece for your places. You're to be out of the valley by the end of the week. That's five days.'

'Well, I'll be damned,' Dollit said in a pleased voice. 'Five hundred dollars! Hear that, Nick? Easiest money a man ever made. Mister, uncork your ink bottle and count out my money.'

Dollit swaggered up the aisle, Nick Bailey behind him. Brad sensed a real difference in the two men. Dollit had undoubtedly been playing Rand's game from the first, but Nick Bailey belonged with the settlers. Whereas Dollit had an assured manner, Bailey had the furtive air of a man who was thoroughly ashamed.

'This is a simple form, Dollit.' Rand pushed a sheet of paper across the desk. 'Just says you're signing over any rights you have to the quarter section you've been claiming.'

Dollit wrote his name and pocketed the gold Rand handed him. Bailey picked up the pen and signed.

Turning her head, Jeanie nodded at Brad. 'Time to start the ball.'

Brad moved toward the front of the room, calling: 'Nick, I didn't figure when the chips were down that you'd sell your saddle like this!'

Bailey grabbed the money Rand was holding out, wheeled, and ran toward the door.

'Wait for me, Nick!' Dollit shouted. 'You ain't got nothing to be ashamed of.' He walked out with what dignity he possessed.

Rand glared at Brad, his eyes wicked. He said: 'Wilder, I aim to keep this peaceable if I can. You can kick hell loose some other time, but right now these folks have a right to get what they can.'

'Well, now,' Brad said, 'I'd just as soon kick hell loose right here as any place. You overlooked one question I aim to have answered. Why haven't you showed us real proof that you own the valley?'

Rand's lips tightened. He nodded at Kinnear, breathing: 'He wants proof, Smoke. Show him some.'

Kinnear stepped away from the desk so that he faced Brad, the characteristic small smile on his lips. 'I've got the proof, Wilder,' he said as he patted his gun butts. 'Two of 'em.'

For a moment there was absolute silence. To Brad, this was the campfire scene all over again. Brad looked into Kinnear's pale, insolent eyes, waiting to see if Kinnear meant business. Again it was Gail who broke it up.

'Riley, pull off your gun dog. I told you to leave him in camp.' She jumped up and ran to the front of the room. 'Folks, I'm Riley's sister and his partner. I don't want any bloodshed on my conscience. That's why I insisted he make this offer.'

'All right, Smoke,' Rand murmured. 'Let it go.'

Kinnear shrugged. 'That's twice she's saved your hide, bucko.'

Brad wheeled to face the settlers. 'It sure

gravels me to hear Rand call Cory a liar and hint he was trying to fill his own pockets. You know Cory too well to believe that.'

Hildreth rose. 'I feel the same way, Brad, but it strikes me that Corey made a mistake. If this comes to a shooting war, I don't want no part of it. One life ain't worth all the damned swampland in the valley.'

'Cory would like to hear you say that,' Brad breathed. 'He told me this morning that you were sound, but, if I'm hearing right, he sure as hell was wrong.'

'We ain't fighting men,' Hildreth said hoarsely, fat cheeks growing red. He motioned to Rand and Kinnnear. 'They are. I say we'd better make the best deal we can.'

'Maybe you want the *dinero* we owe you,' Brad said. 'Five hundred dollars apiece would give us enough to pay our store bill.'

The color in Hildreth's cheeks deepened. 'No, I ain't thinking of that. I just don't want to see good men die for nothing.'

'As far as you're concerned, Mister Hildreth,' Rand said smoothly, 'I won't insist on your leaving the valley. I'll need a store here, so I'll be glad to rent you the land your buildings are on.'

It was a smart move, Brad thought. With Cory absent, Hildreth was as near a leader as the settlers had. Rand was counting on him swinging them over. Brad had a hunch that the whole thing had been planned. Kinnear had never intended to pull his gun. It had simply been a gesture to show the settlers what they would be up against if it came to a fight.

But Hildreth did not take the bait. He said: 'Thank you kindly, Mister Rand, but I'll go with my friends.' Hildreth started toward the table.

Brad said: 'Wait, Tom. I've got one more thing to say. I didn't know till this morning that Cory knew the valley had been marked as swampland. He thought he could buy it himself, and he still thinks he'll get it. When he does, he'll sell the land to you folks and give you all the time you need to pay.'

'I tell you I've already bought the valley,'

Rand said hotly.

Brad still faced the settlers. He saw doubt in their faces, for the trust they had in Cory Steele could not be easily killed. He said: 'Cory expects to hear from Salem any day. We all know there's been some kick about the way the sale of swampland has been handled. Cory promised to settle the valley. That's why he fetched you here. If we hang tight, we'll win.'

'Take my offer or leave it,' Rand said ominously.

'We'll leave it!' Brad shouted. 'I'm trying to say what Cory would say if he was here. Wait a few days. We don't have to sign anything today. If Rand wasn't worried, he wouldn't be trying to stampede us. Let him fetch a U.S. marshal in here to run us out if it comes to that.'

Jeanie was on her feet now, her chin thrust forward defiantly. She said: 'If Dad was here, that's exactly what he'd say. We can't lose anything by waiting, but we can lose all we've got by signing today.'

'Looks to me like Dollit and young Bailey are the only smart men in the crowd!' Rand bellowed. 'You'll lose five hundred dollars apiece if you don't sign today. I ain't gonna hold that offer open.'

'I'm asking you,' Brad flung at them, 'whether Riley Rand looks like the kind of man who'd throw ten thousand dollars away unless he figured he didn't have a real claim to the valley?'

Brad saw he had won. They were talking among themselves, and Rand's threatening words – 'Come on. I ain't wasting all day here. Line up and get your money.' – had no effect on them.

The Widow Bain was on her feet. 'I ain't signing nothing, mister,' she said, and walked out.

'Me, neither!' Rimrock O'Shay shouted. 'Not today I ain't.'

Others rose and followed, not even glancing back at the furious Rand. Nick Bailey's folks went with the others. Only Hildreth waited, unhappy and tormented.

Brad said: 'I thought you were one man who'd back me.'

'All right, Wilder,' Rand said in a low wicked tone. 'What you done today just made some widows and orphans. I'll clear this valley before my herd gets here. That's a promise.'

Hildreth motioned to Brad with a trembling hand. 'You made a mistake today, Brad, a bad one.'

Without a word, Brad turned to Jeanie who was waiting for him. They went down the stairs together, the warm glow of triumph in Brad. He was thinking of things Cory had said. Cory had said it was Jeanie's mother who had changed him. Well, it was Jeanie who had changed Brad Wilder. Cory had been right about something else, too. There was no sense in throwing away the best years of his life. He'd ask Jeanie, and he'd marry her tomorrow if she'd have him.

Brad did not see Gail until he reached the ground. She said: 'Well, Wilder, you pulled it off.'

Jeanie faced Gail, coolly appraising her, and it struck Brad that he had never seen two women who were more different. There was nothing girlish about Jeanie now as she stared contemptuously at Gail Rand.

'I'm proud of him,' Jeanie said. 'I would have been proud of my father if he had been here and said the things Brad said. I never really understood before the things my father likes to say, but I do now.'

'What, for instance?'

'That it is better to die for what you believe in than to live and know you're a coward.'

Gail was amused. 'Tell me one thing, Miss Steele. Have you ever seen a man brought in across his saddle, shot during a range war?'

'No.'

'I didn't think so. I have. It's something you'll remember all your life. Don't let it happen here.'

'Then you stop it!' Jeanie cried. 'I won't.'

'You're young and foolish. Brad Wilder will die, and you'll never forgive yourself for the part you had in killing him.' She looked at Brad. 'You know how it will go, Wilder. You can stop it.'

'I reckon not, miss.'

'*You* stop it!' Jeanie cried again.

'I can't,' Gail said. 'I've done all I can. My brother never lets anyone stop him when he sees something he wants.'

'Come on, Jeanie,' Brad said. 'Let's drift.'

Brad and Jeanie walked toward their horses. Gail stood motionless, genuine concern in her eyes. Brad and Jeanie mounted, and rode away. Gail, Brad thought, had been sincere. He had suspected her of playing a part in her brother's scheming, but now he wasn't sure.

Brad had thought in that one fine moment when he'd left the hall and been filled with the bright glow of triumph that he would tell Jeanie he loved her, but the right words would not come, and they rode back in utter silence, Jeanie's face somber and clouded by worry.

They reached the Steele place in early evening with purple shadow clinging to the western rim, the last of the day's sunlight bright upon the eastern half of the valley. Jeanie said: 'Stay for supper, Brad. Dad will want to hear all about it.'

'Glad to. I reckon Cory will be happy about the way it turned out.'

'Yes, he will,' Jeanie said, and went into the house.

Brad led the horses toward the log trough, but before he reached it, he heard Jeanie's scream, shrill and terrible with horror. He dropped the reins and ran into the cabin. Jeanie was standing just inside the doorway, her eyes on her father. He lay in the middle of the room, sightless eyes staring upward, his gun a foot from an outstretched hand.

Stooping, Brad felt of Cory's wrist. There was no flicker of a pulse. He had died just as he had expected to. There was a bullet hole in his chest.

Chapter Three

Brad did not know how long he stood there, staring at Cory Steele's body, nor did he know how Jeanie got into his arms, but she was there, crying, and Brad held her as he might have held a child, comforting her. But at this moment for Brad Wilder, it was as if the sun had suddenly refused to shine, and the darkness was all around. In a way Cory Steele had been like an older brother to Brad. He had said frankly he was a leader, but he had not bragged about it. It had been a simple statement of truth. Now he was dead, and those who followed had no one to look to.

Cory Steele had not been at the meeting in person, but it had been his spirit that had beaten Riley Rand. Rand must have sensed the strength that was in Cory even though he was an invalid held within the walls of his cabin. So he had ordered Cory's murder, thinking it would take the heart out of the settlers' resistance.

Without a word Brad led Jeanie into the thinning sunlight. He said: 'You can't stay here. We'll go back to Hildreth's.'

She gripped his arm. 'Brad, who did it?'

He knew, but he looked away from her. 'Who do you think?'

'Everyone stayed till the end of the meeting except Nick Bailey and Whang Dollit,' she said tonelessly.

Brad shook his head. He did not answer.

'Then it *was* Nick.'

'Or Dollit.'

She looked westward across the valley where the sun was showing a red arc above the rimrock. 'He knew this was coming, and I was impatient with him. I thought he was just tired of being laid up, but he knew, Brad. He *knew*.'

It was dark by the time they started back to

Getalong, Cory's body wrapped in canvas in the back of the wagon. The cabin had been ransacked, and Cory's saddle horse had been stolen. Brad had made a careful search around the house and barn, but he had been unable to pick up a clue that would identify the murderer. There was no doubt in his mind about it, and he was sure that everyone except Nick Bailey's parents would reach the same conclusion.

'They'll come back and burn our place, won't they?' Jeanie asked suddenly. 'It's all part of Rand's scheme to clear the valley, isn't it?'

It was likely, Brad thought, that they would do exactly that.

'They wanted it to look like robbery, didn't they?' Jeanie asked.

'I guess so.'

They rode in silence, then, the darkness pressing around them. A light showed in the window of the Widow Bain's cabin. Later they could see Rimrock O'Shay's light, a tiny pin prick in a vast sea of black space.

Once Brad heard Jeanie sob, but he thought it was better to leave her alone. There was nothing anybody could say, now, that would help. Death was not a new thing to him.

Brad wondered what would happen next. The settlers had defied Rand because they had expected Cory to get back on his feet; they had believed what Brad had said about Cory's buying the valley and selling their land to them. Now, he thought, they would drift away, and that was exactly what Rand expected.

Finally they pulled up in front of Hildreth's house. The door swung open, and yellow light fell through the opening in a long finger. Hildreth called in worried tones: 'Who is it?'

'Brad. Jeanie's here, too.'

'What brings you back?'

Brad stepped down from the wagon seat as Hildreth moved ponderously across the yard to them. Brad lifted Jeanie down as Hildreth came up, peering questioningly at them in the darkness.

'Cory was murdered this afternoon,' Brad said.

Hildreth stopped dead. Mrs Hildreth had come out of the house in time to hear what Brad said. She began to shriek, a strange, incoherent, unnerving sound.

Hildreth wheeled on her. 'Liza, I've never struck you, but if you don't stop that, I will.'

She covered her face with her apron and ran into the house.

Brad said: 'I thought you could take Jeanie in. She can't stay there.'

'Of course. Come in, Jeanie. I'll get a lantern.'

Hildreth walked to the house. Jeanie hesitated a moment, her hand gripping Brad's arm. 'Don't let them kill you, Brad,' she whispered. 'We need you. You know what Dad expected of you.'

It was something he had been thinking about all the way in. He had thought that it was a job he could not do. Now he knew he had to do that job. Just how, he did not know. 'My hide's bullet-proof. I wish there was something I could say.'

'I know, Brad. There's nothing. He's gone. That's all. You're all I've got now, and I couldn't bear losing you, too, but I know what has to be done.'

Turning, she walked quickly into the house, her head high. He watched her disappear inside. She had said: *You're all I've got now.* He knew then that she loved him and wondered why he had not known it all the time. Still, loving him, she had not said: *Let's ride away. You may be killed if we stay.*

Hildreth came out of the house, a lighted lantern in his hand. He said hoarsely: 'Drive around to the back of the store.'

Brad stepped into the seat, Hildreth following, and Brad drove past the store building and swung in behind it. Hildreth got down and opened the door. He hung the lantern on a nail, and turned back.

'We'll leave him here,' Hildreth said. 'I'll sit up with him tonight. Looks like we'll be busy for a few days, so we'd best bury him tomorrow. I'll make the coffin in the morning while you're getting word to everybody.'

They carried the body inside.

Hildreth wiped a sleeve across his eyes. He said: 'It's queer, the way you get to feeling about somebody. Seemed like Cory was immortal. I never thought of his dying.'

'What will folks do now?' Brad mused. 'Folks counted a heap on Cory. Now he's gone.'

Hildreth lowered his gaze. 'Rand figured wrong on this. So have you. Cory is going to be bigger dead than he was alive. We won't run, Brad.' Hildreth swallowed. 'Cut any sign on the killing sons-of-bitches that done it?'

'No.'

'Well, don't make no difference. Dollit and Nick Bailey will have a bad time explaining where they went after they left here.'

'I don't figure we'll ever see 'em again.'

'We'll see 'em, all right. Rand needs their guns. Dollit's, anyhow.' Hildreth scratched his bald head. 'I can't believe Nick had a hand in it. He ain't much good, but he ain't a killer.'

Brad said nothing, but he did not share Hildreth's faith in young Bailey. 'Got another lantern?' he asked. 'I'll put the horses away.'

'There's one hanging just inside the barn door.'

Brad's horse had been tied behind the wagon. He untied him now and unhooked the team. He put them and Jeanie's saddle horse away, and returned to the store. He said: 'I'll stop at Rimrock's place and send him in. He can spell you off so you can get a little sleep.'

'Where are you goin' to stay?'

'Cory's place. Jeanie's afraid they'll burn the cabin.'

Hildreth gripped Brad's arm. 'You can't do that. Rand's next move will be to get you. Then where'll we be?'

Brad looked at Hildreth's bearded face. Indirectly Hildreth had said the same thing Cory had said a few hours before. *It's up to you.* For the first time in his life Brad felt the weight that Cory Steele had carried for years, the faith and trust of other men. Silently

Brad mounted and rode away, leaving Hildreth standing under the lantern and staring anxiously after him.

It took Brad all the next morning to circle the lake and tell the settlers about Cory's death and the funeral. With one exception they received the news the same way. They were shocked. The Baileys were the only ones who varied the pattern. Old man Bailey stood in front of his cabin, the wind riffling his long white hair. His wife was behind him, a tight-lipped little woman with faded sad eyes. Brad felt pity for them. Nick, he had heard, was their only child.

'Who done it?' Bailey asked.

He was the first to ask that question, and Brad found himself looking away toward the wind-tossed surface of the lake. He said: 'I don't know.'

'But you think you know,' Bailey said, 'and I think I know. I ain't seen Nick since the meeting yesterday. Now I'll tell you something. If you bring Nick and Dollit in, I'll help hang them both.'

Mrs Bailey cried out and gripped his arm. 'No, Paul, no!'

But the old man nodded, the agony of shame in him. 'For years he's brought us nothing but trouble. There's only one way to deal with a man when he joins a wolf pack. We'll treat him that way whether he's my son or not.'

'Maybe it won't come to that,' Brad said, and rode away.

The settlers had begun to gather in Getalong by the time Brad completed the circle. He ate dinner in Hildreth's kitchen, Mrs Hildreth waiting on him in her silent, distant way, her eyes disapproving when they settled on his gun. Brad did not see Jeanie, but he could hear the hum of low, mournful talk that flowed in from the parlor.

Brad rose when he finished eating, shaking his head at Mrs Hildreth's offer of more coffee. She came toward him then, her thin face very pale. She said: 'They're all talking about you now, Mister Wilder. Because you carry a gun, they think you'll take Cory Steele's place.'

'I reckon you're wrong, ma'am,' Brad said quietly. 'Nobody can take Cory's place.'

'They're talking about revenge,' she breathed. 'About hanging Dollit and young Bailey and maybe this Riley Rand, but that means fighting. Our men will be killed. Will it bring Cory Steele back?'

He looked at her, wondering if she had been responsible for Hildreth's attitude during the meeting. Brad could not argue with her. He had seen this happen many times before, the women crying for peace and never considering the price of that peace. 'You've been listening to Gail Rand,' Brad said. 'We have to do what we have to do.' He pulled away from her grip and left the room.

The grave was not quite finished, and Brad took a shovel and spelled Rimrock O'Shay. By the time it was done, the coffin had been built and lined with black cloth from the store. More wagons were coming in. Before two o'clock every settler in the valley was in Getalong for the second successive day.

The women gravitated toward the house, the men to the rear of the store. They made a solid knot in front of Brad, their eyes expectant. Hildreth said: 'It's a little while before we start the service. We'd best decide what to do.'

O'Shay threw a hand out toward Brad. 'You knew Cory better'n any of us, I reckon. What would he tell us to do?'

Brad hesitated. If any of them died, it would be his responsibility, and the women would hate him as long as they lived. Tight-lipped, Brad said: 'You're handing me quite a chore.'

'We know that,' Hildreth said, 'but you're the only one who can handle it. I'm thanking you for keeping me from doing something yesterday that I'd have been ashamed of all my life. I honestly thought Rand owned the valley. If he did, our fighting would be wasted.'

'You still don't know Rand wasn't telling

the truth.'

Hildreth spread his fat hands. 'We know all right. If he'd been telling the truth, he wouldn't have had Cory killed.'

The rest nodded, and Brad understood what Hildreth had meant the night before when he'd said that Cory would be bigger dead than he had been alive. 'There's only one thing to do that I can see,' Brad said thoughtfully. 'It means some fighting. Maybe some of you will be lying here beside Cory before the week's over.'

'We know that,' Rimrock O'Shay said with some heat. 'I was talking crazy yesterday when I said I didn't want no fighting on account of I've got a wife and kids.' He looked past Brad at the open grave. 'If Riley Rand gets the valley, there'll be a lot of graves yonder.'

There was a murmur of agreement. Even old man Bailey, standing far back in the crowd, showed he'd go along. Brad knew then they would do what Cory wanted. They'd hang and rattle. 'All right,' Brad said.

'Here's what we'll do. Rand said he'd give us five days, but I doubt that he will. He'll be mighty sore because we didn't take his proposition yesterday, so I'm guessing he'll do something like dry-gulching us or burning our cabins. Maybe run our cattle out of the valley.'

'Well, then,' O'Shay said, 'We'd better hit him first.'

'That's my idea,' Brad said. 'Soon as the funeral's over we'll go after Dollit. If we find him, we'll give him a trial and hang him. Then we'll shove Rand and his wagons through the notch and tell him to stay out of the valley. We'll put men around the rim and fix some piles of brush for signal fires. If Rand comes back, we'll kill him. While we're gone, you'd better leave your wives and kids here.'

'Say,' Al Benton said sourly, 'if we do that, they'll burn every cabin in the valley while we're lookin' for 'em.'

'There's a chance they might do that,' Brad agreed, 'but we've got to count on losing something. I'll tell you another thing, Al. Rand claims he's got a herd on the trail. He's probably got ten men, maybe more, with his cattle. If he sends for his bunch, we'll have a fight. But they can't handle us if we get the jump on 'em. We'll wait till dark. Rand won't expect us to hit him.'

'Soon as the funeral's over,' O'Shay said, 'we'll head for home and do our chores, then strike south.'

'I'll get a small fire going in the pocket,' Brad said. 'That's close to Rand's camp, but they can't see us. We'll gather there.'

Hildreth glanced at his watch. 'Time for the service.'

It was a simple service. There was no preacher in the valley, and no time to send to Canon City for one, so Hildreth read from the Bible and prayed.

In the little cemetery later, Jeanie stood very straight with the Widow Bain's arm around her, as the coffin was slowly lowered into the grave. Then the widow led her away, and Brad picked up a shovel and helped fill the grave.

They broke up then. Brad saw that most of the wagons were leaving without the women and children. Brad saddled and rode around the store, and, when he passed the house, he saw Jeanie on the porch. She waved, and walked down the path to him. He reined up, wondering what he could say to her.

Jeanie smiled when she came up, a small curve of her lips. She said: 'Brad, there was a lot about Dad's past he never told anyone but me. But all the time since I can remember, he's been a good man. I didn't sleep any last night. Maybe I imagined this, but it seemed to me he was in the room, talking to me. That's why I didn't cry today. The grief I feel is for myself. I think Dad is very happy.'

He saw that there was no real sadness in her face, and it surprised him. He had been wrong in thinking tears would help. Not Jeanie Steele. There was nothing girlish about her now. These last few days had matured her.

'Don't go back to your place,' Brad said.

'I won't,' she promised. 'Not till this is over. Take care of yourself, Brad.'

'I figure on doing that,' he said, and rode away.

The sun had dipped toward the west, its sharp glare upon the valley, but the wind was still bitter. *A good day for Cory's funeral,* Brad thought. Then he lowered his gaze to the wheel ruts that ran ahead of him, and the weight of reality became a load upon him.

Brad was the first to reach the pocket, a shallow cave in the rock wall a mile east of the Rand camp. He was out of the wind here, but it was still cold. He built a fire and held his hands out to it, and grew impatient with the waiting, but there was nothing to do for a time.

They began drifting in presently, Rimrock O'Shay and Al Benton and some others, riding singly and making a wide swing across the sage flat. If Rand had run into any of them, they could have said they were out looking for cattle, but neither Rand nor

Kinnear had been seen. The Rand campfire, O'Shay reported, looked like a house burning down. It was that big.

Uneasiness touched Brad. A fire that big was wasteful, and Rand, Brad judged, was not a man who would be wasteful of anything without a purpose. Perhaps the fire marked an empty camp, intended to lull the settlers into a sense of security. There was something else, too, that surprised Brad and added to his uneasiness. Anger had grown in these men since the funeral until now it was a cold revengeful rage. Their talk was wild, and impatience prodded them. They wanted to hang everybody they caught, including Gail Rand.

'It ain't good enough just to run them Rands out of the valley,' O'Shay cried. 'They'll come back with their tough hands and wipe us out.'

'Maybe, but hanging a man is mighty permanent,' Brad said quietly. 'Cory believed in a lot of things that were good for the valley. One was law. He said we had to avoid anything that would give us a bad name.'

'Bad name!' O'Shay bellowed. 'We'll have a bad name if we let this go!'

'We won't let it go,' Brad said. 'I told you we'd try Dollit, if we find him. Nick Bailey, too. If they killed Cory, we'll hang 'em, but we've got no hanging charge against the rest.'

O'Shay's eyes dropped under the pressure of Brad's stare, but he remained sullen and unconvinced. A few hours before, O'Shay and the others had been meek enough, uncertain whether to fight or run, but now they were filled with a lust to kill that only Cory Steele's murder could have aroused in them.

There were fifteen men standing around a fire. Studying them, Brad saw the same sullen rage on every weather-burned face from Rimrock O'Shay's grizzled one to that of Al Benton who was the mildest man in the valley.

'Hildreth said he'd stay till dusk in case the mail got in,' Brad said. 'We'll have to wait for him, but I think I'll take a sashay over to Rand's camp just to see how the land lies. You boys stay here.'

They nodded, saying nothing, but Brad wasn't sure they'd obey. He turned toward his horse and mounted, thinking how much these men had changed. At least, they had changed in temper and resolve, but what they'd do when the shooting started was something else. Riley Rand obviously thought that one man like Smoke Kinnear was worth ten settlers, and Brad wondered if Rand was wrong.

Brad rode away, making a wide turn through the sagebrush so that he would come into Rand's camp from the north. A shot rang out, suddenly and without warning. Brad reined up, wondering if he had been seen. Then he realized that the shot had not been intended for him. It had been some distance to the north. He rode on, puzzled about it and unable to quiet the worry in him. Kinnear or Dollit might have met up with one of the settlers, Hildreth perhaps, and shot him down. If that'd happened, there would be no holding the men at the fire.

The Rand fire was still too big. Covered by darkness, Brad reined up and sat his saddle for a few moments, watching. George McCloud was there. So was the Chinese cook. Apparently everyone else was gone, although it was quite likely that Gail was in her tent.

Again worry gnawed at Brad's nerves. He had thought Rand and his men would be here. If they intended to strike tonight, they would likely be in camp now, waiting until the small hours before dawn to make their raid. Now Brad saw that he had guessed wrong. To go back and get the settlers and then start hunting for Rand would be both futile and foolish. If only there was some way to find out exactly what Rand was planning... An idea struck Brad. George McCloud might know, and he was a man who could be made to talk.

Dismounting, Brad moved silently toward the fire. The cook was working at the chuck wagon. McCloud was idling by the fire, round-cheeked face untouched by worry or fear. He probably thought he was on a picnic, Brad thought. Maybe he wouldn't know. He didn't look like the kind of man who would have a part in Rand's scheming.

Brad moved in, gun palmed. McCloud heard him as he came into the firelight. He jumped up and whirled to face Brad, right hand grabbing for a gun in a shoulder holster.

'Stand pat,' Brad ordered.

McCloud's hand fell away, and he began to curse in a low scared voice.

He knows, Brad thought. *He's into this up to his neck.*

At the moment Brad was watching McCloud, and it was exactly that moment when the Chinese cook wheeled and threw a butcher knife, the blade a bright flash of silver in the firelight. It missed by inches, and, when the cook saw he'd failed, he began to yell for mercy.

'Chang good now,' he whimpered. 'Belly good.'

'You're darn' tootin' right you'll be good,' Brad said angrily. 'You make another funny move and I'll cut off your pigtail at your neck. Savvy?'

The cook bobbed his head up and down.

Brad motioned to McCloud. 'Pull your gun and drop it. Try to use it and you'll be a goner.'

Sullenly McCloud drew his gun and tossed it away.

Brad moved close to him. He said: 'I'll have a look for a hide-out, friend. You ain't as harmless as you look.'

Brad felt of McCloud with his left hand, right holding his gun, but there was no other weapon on the man. McCloud stood motionless, frowning with apprehension. When Brad stepped back, he demanded: 'What do you want?'

'I'm looking for Rand and his bunch. Where are they?'

'I don't know.'

'Who fired that shot I heard a while ago?'

'I don't know.'

'When did Rand and his boys ride out?'

'About an hour ago.'

'Gail go with them?'

'Yes.'

'You knew that Cory Steele was murdered?'

'Nick Bailey said something about it.'

'Nick do it?'

'I don't know.'

'You don't know very much, do you?' Brad asked angrily.

McCloud shook his head. 'That's right. I don't ask Rand about his plans.'

'Maybe you know what you're doing here?'

Courage had drained back into McCloud now. He gave Brad a defiant grin. 'Sure. I came to see the country. I'll tell you one thing, Wilder. Gail knows she made a mistake when she stopped Kinnear from shooting you the other night. She's just too soft-hearted for Riley. He's about ready to ship her back to Winnemucca, and then he'll clean this valley out.'

'Maybe he'll ship you, too.'

'Not me. I don't worry anybody. By fall I'll be ready to go back East and tell my friends some stories that will brand me the biggest liar on this side of the Atlantic.'

'If you live long enough to go back,' Brad said. 'Maybe you *are* the biggest liar on this side of the Atlantic. What's Rand up to tonight?'

'I said I didn't know anything about it.'

There was a chance Rand's bunch might ride in, and Brad didn't want to be caught here alone. He said: 'I'm mighty sure you ain't here just to see the country. I'm taking you along. Saddle up.'

'Now see here, my man...'

Brad motioned with his gun. 'Don't think I'm your man, friend. You ain't in New York now. Saddle up.'

For a moment McCloud stared at the gun in Brad's hand. He said: 'I think you would kill me just like you'd shoot a ... a...'

'Rabbit,' Brad said. 'You're right, I would. Before the night's over you'll swing that tongue of yours, or I'll pull it out of your head. Move now.'

McCloud obeyed, Brad backing away so

that he could watch both the cook and Mc-Cloud. When the saddle was on and the cinch tightened, Brad said: 'Climb up. My horse is out here a piece. Was I you, I wouldn't try to make a run for it. I shoot awful good in the dark.'

McCloud made no answer. He rode slowly away from the fire, Brad walking beside him until he reached his horse. He said: 'Pull up.'

'Where we going?'

'Some of Cory Steele's friends are waiting a piece east of here. They've got ropes for Dollit and Nick Bailey, but maybe your neck will fit one of the loops.'

'You wouldn't do that. It would be murder.'

'We've had a murder, and the man who got it was a better man than you'll ever be. All I want from you is a little talk.'

'You forget who I am. My brother...'

'It makes no difference if your brother is the king of Siam. Where's Rand?'

'I don't know.'

Brad was in the saddle now, his gun still palmed. 'Let's ride, and, while you're riding, you'd better do some thinking.'

They rode eastward, McCloud saying nothing. There was a sort of sullen courage in him that surprised Brad, but he still thought the man would break. They came within sight of the fire in the pocket and turned toward it. As they rode into the light, the settlers crowded around him.

'Who's this yahoo?' O'Shay demanded.

'Calls himself McCloud. Says he's got a brother who's a big gun in the East, so we've got to go easy on him.'

Al Benton laughed. 'That's a good reason to go easy. What'd you fetch him along for, Brad?'

'Nobody was in camp but McCloud and the Chinese cook. I figured this jigger would know what Rand's up to.'

There was a moment of shocked silence while they stared at Brad. He sensed the rising fear in them as they realized that Rand and his men were somewhere out in the valley. Benton whispered: 'I didn't leave my family at Getalong like you said. They're all in my cabin. You reckon Rand aims to...?'

'You fool,' Brad said angrily. 'You feather-headed fool! I told you...'

'Wait a minute, Brad,' O'Shay cut in. 'Somebody's coming.'

Brad stepped down. 'Stay there, McCloud. Everybody else get away from the fire.'

They obeyed and stood motionless just outside the fringe of firelight while they waited, guns in their hands.

For that one tight moment there was no sound but the crackling of the fire and the whisper of horses' hoofs. McCloud sat his saddle beside the fire, paralyzed by fear, his round-cheeked face as pale as a dawn sky. Then Hildreth rode into view leading a horse, a man swaying in the saddle, and a whoop came out of half a dozen throats as tension drained out of the men.

'Why didn't you give a holler?' O'Shay called. 'You just about had us spooked.'

Then they saw that the other man was Nick Bailey, and they crowded up, Brad asking: 'Where'd you find him?'

'He's hit bad,' Hildreth said. 'Heard him holler a couple of miles north of here. Found him lying in the grass. Dollit plugged him. Figured he'd killed him, I reckon.'

Brad and Benton helped Bailey down and carried him to the fire. He'd been shot in the stomach and blood had made a dark stain on his shirt front. His eyes were open, and they fixed on Brad, empty now of the jealous hatred they had so often held when he'd looked at Brad. His face was a ghastly gray, and, when he coughed, a bloody froth touched his lips. He was very close to death.

Brad brought a saddle and blanket, lifted Bailey's head, and slid the saddle under it, then covered him with the blanket. Brad motioned for McCloud to get down. 'Stay there,' Brad ordered. 'Savvy?'

McCloud stepped down, nodding, and moved to the other side of the fire. Bailey reached up and touched Brad's leg. He whispered: 'Dad here?'

Kneeling beside Bailey, Brad said: 'No.'

'I'm glad. You figured on hanging me,

didn't you, and you didn't want him to see it?'

'That's right, Nick,' Hildreth said, kneeling on the other side of the dying man.

'Funny,' Bailey whispered. 'Now that it's too late, I can see a lot of things I never could before. Tell Dad I'm sorry for all the worry I caused him. Tell him I didn't kill Cory. Dollit did.'

'Why?' Brad asked.

'Rand sent Dollit here last fall to spy on everybody. He's had his eyes on this valley for quite a while, but he had trouble raising the money. Then they met up with McCloud. Rand had the *dinero* then, but he ran into trouble in Salem making the deal.' For a moment Bailey was silent, fighting the weakness that was taking hold of him. Then he said: 'I'm cold. Inside.' He clenched his fists, and looked at Brad. 'I've hated you on account of Jeanie. She's loved you all the time. Maybe I never had a chance with her. Just thought I did. Dollit came along. Offered me a fortune to side him. That's why I sold out yesterday. Rand thought that, if two of us started it, everybody would sell out.' His eyes closed.

Brad motioned to Benton. 'Toss some more wood on the fire. He's shivering.'

Benton obeyed, and a flame leaped up.

Bailey's eyes opened and sought Hildreth's face. 'You've got to fight, Tom. Rand don't own the valley like he claims. Cory's deal went through. Dollit shot the mailman. That's why he never got in. There was a letter to Cory.'

'We'll fight, Nick,' Hildreth said softly. 'You bet we'll fight.'

'I didn't know Dollit aimed to beef Cory,' Bailey went on. 'He shot him before I saw what he was up to. Rand wanted Cory out of the way. Dollit told Rand that Cory and Wilder were the only ones who'd fight. Rand was awful mad at Gail for stopping Kinnear from killing Wilder. Next time they'll get him.'

Bailey's eyes closed again, and for a moment Brad thought he was gone. Then he saw that Bailey was still breathing. His eyes fluttered open, and for a moment they moved wildly. 'Wilder? You there? It's dark. I can't see you.'

'I'm here.' Brad laid a hand on Bailey's arm. 'Right here.'

'You've got to ride. Rand aims to burn some cabins tonight. He went loco after the meeting fizzled out. He'll kill anybody who tries to stop him. He's gonna burn the store, too. I couldn't stand it no longer. He'd have murdered my folks, too. I tried to stop 'em. Dollit ... drilled ... me.' Bailey tried to say something more, but the words would not come. He coughed, and blood was a bright red stain on his lips. 'I deserved what I got.' His eyes were open, but they were staring unseeingly at the sky. 'Wilder. It's awful dark. You there?'

'I'm still here.'

'Take good care of Jeanie. Tell ... my ... folks...'

That was all he could say. Brad felt of his wrist, but there was no flicker of a pulse.

Brad drew the blanket over his face and rose. 'You knew him better than I did, Tom. He couldn't go all the way with Dollit.'

The men stirred. O'Shay said: 'We've got some riding to do, Brad.'

Brad nodded, eyes swinging around the half circle of men and coming to rest on McCloud who was still standing on the other side of the fire as if he had been frozen there. 'You heard what he said about your giving Rand the money to buy the valley. That right?'

'Go chase yourself,' McCloud said sullenly.

Brad drew his gun. 'We ain't got time to fuss with you. I want an answer.'

McCloud glanced down at Bailey's blanket-covered body, his mouth twitching. Then he raised his eyes to Brad. 'Sure, that's right. It's my money Rand used to buy the herd that's coming up the trail, and it was my money he was going to use to buy the valley, but he won't need it now. We'll use the valley regardless.'

Brad holstered his gun, and swung to the

others. 'Tom, you and Malone fetch Bailey's body in. The rest of us have got to split the breeze getting to the store.'

'Our families are there!' O'Shay cried. 'If Rand...'

'Stop worrying,' Brad said. 'Old man Bailey's there. I don't know about the rest of the women, but Jeanie's a good shot. Let's ride.'

'My family went home,' Al Benton whispered. He grabbed Brad's shoulder, pointing north with his other hand to a finger of flame that was leaping skyward. 'Fire! That's my cabin.'

Chapter Four

There was a flurry of action, tightening cinches, and mounting and reining horses away from the fire. There were bitter oaths and angry threats from men who had never been filled with a killing rage as they were now. At the moment danger lay miles away across the valley. They were not yet face to face with it. It would be different when they were, for in the end numbers would not make much difference. One man like Smoke Kinnear could stare the lot of them down. In spite of their talk, Brad was the one who would finally have to do the job. Cory, Brad thought, had foreseen that from the first.

Mounting, Brad called: 'Rimrock, you ride with McCloud. We're going to need him before the night's over. See he don't get behind.'

'I'm not a good rider,' McCloud cried. 'I can't keep up...!'

'You'll keep up,' O'Shay bawled, 'or you'll be laying belly down out in the sagebrush!'

Most of the settlers were already strung out toward the lake. Brad touched his horse up and came alongside Al Benton who was in the lead. The distance between Brad and Benton in front and the others behind gradually widened.

'Slow up!' Brad shouted. 'You'll kill your horse the way you're riding.'

'I don't care if I do,' Benton shouted back in a ragged voice. 'My wife and kids...'

'Rand's ornery, but he ain't a woman-killer.'

'You don't know...'

'Take another look, Al. I'm guessing it's my cabin we're seeing.'

Brad could not be sure at this distance, but Benton must have found relief in the thought, for he pulled his gelding down to a slower pace. They rode steadily toward the blaze across the long sweep of the valley that dropped gently northward, then they were out of the sagebrush and crossing the low flat that bordered the tule-fringed lake, moist soil that would, by fall, be covered with grass belly high on a horse. Cow paradise, just as Rand had said.

Brad thought of the women and children in Hildreth's house with only old Bailey to defend them. A few of the boys were old enough to use guns. Jeanie would do her part. He thought of Jeanie wounded, perhaps dying, and suddenly he was filled with a cold, relentless purpose that would carry him straight to Riley Rand.

Al Benton's voice beat against Brad's ears: 'You're right. It's your place.'

A few minutes later they reined up in Brad's yard and sat their saddles, staring at the smoldering coals that had been a cabin. It'd taken a lot of work to build that cabin and the few pieces of crude furniture. Everything was gone except the clothes Brad had on.

Benton cursed in a low, flat tone, but Brad felt little emotion. This was a minor thing. The big job waited to be done, and time was running out. Others rode in now and reined up to blow their horses. Brad hipped around in his saddle, calling: 'McCloud, this your idea?'

'No.'

'You said it was your investment that fetched Rand up here. Don't you call the turn?'

'No. Rand bargained for a free hand before we left Winnemucca. I told you I just came for the trip.'

'Then you're a damned fool to put your money out and let the other fellow blow it the way he wants to.'

'Maybe I am,' McCloud shouted, 'but Riley promised me a ranch! A big ranch! An empire! You understand? The way he carries out his promise is his business.'

'An empire,' Brad breathed. 'A swampland empire, and you'll wear the crown. That's it, ain't it, McCloud?'

'That's it.'

'Before we're done, maybe we *will* hang you. Al, hike out for home. There's enough of us to do this chore without you.'

Without a word Benton whirled his horse and rode westward around the lake. Brad reined the other way, half expecting flames to burst up from the Steele cabin, but when he saw a fire a few minutes later, it was the Widow Bain's place, not the Steele cabin. Rand, Brad guessed, had saved Jeanie's place because it was the best house in the valley. It was likely that Rand planned to use it as the headquarters of McCloud's ranch until a bigger place could be built.

Rand had ridden past four cabins tonight and burned three. He intended to wipe Hildreth out, confident that the settlers, understanding the kind of man they were up against, would run. If they were still stubborn, their cattle would go. If that didn't work, there would be more killings. Gail, Brad thought, had lost any influence she'd ever held over her brother. If Rand lived, there could be no turning back for him.

Getalong was directly ahead. It would not have surprised Brad to have seen Hildreth's buildings burning. But there was no light to brighten the blackness except that from a lamp in the back of Hildreth's house.

One moment there was silence except for the usual night sounds, then gunfire broke out, a single burst, and after that a man's shout.

Exultation swept through Brad. Riley

Rand had run into more than he had bargained for. Old man Bailey and the women and kids were fighting. Rand had made a wrong guess, perhaps a fatal one, when he had taken the settlers so lightly. He should have had an army of gunslingers instead of just Smoke Kinnear and Whang Dollit. Courage, like gold, is where you find it, and the men coming behind Brad might be encouraged by this show of strength in a way Rand had not counted on.

He was close to Hildreth's house now, calling: 'It's Brad! Hold your fire!'

The back door swung open. Lamplight spilled out across the grass. The Widow Bain cried: 'Hurry, Brad, hurry. We've been looking for you.'

Brad pulled his sweat-gummed horse to a stop and swung down. There were a number of women and several children in the back of the house, and the fury grew in him. What a hell of a thing this was – Rand's endangering the lives of these people.

They were a scared lot. Only the Widow

Bain seemed self-possessed. She patted Brad's shoulder, saying: 'You're a sight for sore eyes, boy. You can take over the fighting now, and welcome to it.'

'Where're the others?' a woman cried. 'Where's my husband?'

'Everybody's all right.'

Brad pushed through the crowd, seeking Jeanie, but she wasn't here. The widow kept close behind him, saying: 'If it hadn't been for Jeanie, we'd have walked out of here, and Rand would have burned everything, but that Jeanie's just like her dad. She's a fighter right down to her toes.'

Brad went on to the front room. Old man Bailey was there with a bloody rag tied around his head. The oldest Bain kid was crouched behind a window, a six-gun in his hand, left arm in a sling. Then Brad saw Jeanie near another window, a Winchester in her hands, blood streaming down her face from an open gash on her cheek.

'Jeanie!' Brad cried. 'Jeanie.'

When she saw it was Brad, a light burst

across her face. 'Brad!'

She dropped the Winchester and ran to him. He put his arms around her and held her close.

'Brad, are you all right?'

'Sure. Those yahoos gave us the slip. I figured we'd find them in camp. Looks like we should have stayed right here.'

She wiped a hand across her face. 'A piece of glass from the window gave me a scratch. Nobody's hurt badly.'

He looked at the gash. 'Pretty deep.' He nodded at the Widow Bain. 'Better clean this up. May leave a scar.'

'It doesn't matter,' Jeanie said impatiently. 'They've been threatening to rush us. They're holed up in the store.'

'They've got a bear by the tail now.' Brad grinned at her. 'They won't do any rushing. You know what you've done tonight?'

'Done?' She shook her head. 'We haven't done anything.'

'You've done quite a chore,' Brad said. 'You've showed Rand that women and kids and one old man will fight. He can't lick us now, Jeanie, not in a million years. I wish Cory could see this.'

Jeanie said gravely: 'He's right here with us. If he hadn't been, we'd have quit when they rode up.'

Some of the men were riding in. They crowded into the kitchen, O'Shay keeping his gun on McCloud.

'Damn that Rand!' O'Shay bellowed. 'He burned our cabin. Everything we own went up in smoke. Burned yours, too, Missus Bain.'

Mrs O'Shay began to cry hysterically, but the Widow Bain only spread her hands and said: 'Then we'll have to build again.'

O'Shay prodded McCloud in the back with his gun. 'You'll pay us for every bit of devilment this Rand *hombre* has done since he hit the valley.'

Old man Bailey pushed his way into the crowded kitchen, calling: 'Nick, Nick? He wasn't with Rand's bunch. Have any of you seen him?'

Hildreth could have told him if he were here, but Hildreth would not be in for hours, so Brad told the old man as gently as he could, adding: 'I can't blame him for hating me or loving Jeanie. He took the wrong road, but when the last chip was down, he found out he couldn't go all the way with Dollit.'

Mrs Bailey was crying, but the old man drew himself erect, a defiant pride in his eye. 'If Nick had to die, I'm glad he went that way. He didn't forget his people.'

'That's right,' Brad said.

'What's going on here?' O'Shay demanded imperiously. 'Who's in the store?'

'Rand and his sister,' Jeanie said. 'Dollit and that gunman Kinnear are with them. They rode up in front and told us to get out of the house. They said they were going to burn the house and the store.'

'You know why we didn't go?' the Widow Bain demanded. 'Because Jeanie wouldn't let us. She grabbed a Winchester and put a hole through Rand's bonnet. You should have seen 'em scurry.'

'They came through the back of the store,' Jeanie said, 'and now they're forted up behind the front windows. About every half hour Rand has been asking us if we're ready to get out.'

'You men are here.' The Widow Bain motioned toward the store. 'Six, seven, eight of you with Bailey. Go run 'em out and get this over with.'

No one moved. O'Shay shifted uneasily. 'You're forgetting one thing, Missus Bain. Them three in there are mighty tough hands. They'd cut us down before we got halfway across the yard.'

'There's enough of us to do the job,' Brad said. 'It's still dark. We could get to the front door of the store, all right.'

'Suppose we did?' O'Shay asked loudly. 'We'd go in and they'd be in the dark and what light there is would be behind us. We'd be targets for 'em.'

They wouldn't back him. They had blown hot and cold, and now they were cold. Knowing that Cory Steele's murderer was in the store and knowing that three cabins had been burned this night, the fury had died in them.

'I'm ashamed of you,' Jeanie cried. 'You know what Dad would do if he was here.'

'And you know what Brad will do now,' the Widow Bain said in high contempt. 'Come on, Brad. Give me your gun, Rimrock. I'll side him.'

'I'll go,' Bailey said quickly.

'It won't do!' O'Shay shouted. 'No use getting burned down for nothing. We'll wait 'em out.'

'We can't do that,' Brad said. 'It's almost dawn now. Unless we bottle 'em up in the store, they'll ride out after a while. Then we'd have to run 'em down again. This is the best chance we'll ever have.'

McCloud laughed. 'You're a bunch of fools to think you could lick Rand. You know what he said?'

'I don't care what he said!' O'Shay shouted defiantly. 'We'll sit him out.'

'I'll tell you,' McCloud went on. 'When Dollit told us how it stacked up here in the valley, Riley said Smoke Kinnear was worth all of you. Burn a few cabins, throw a flew slugs, and you'd run like chickens when a hawk flies over the barnyard.'

'Damn you!' O'Shay slapped the man across the face. 'You'd like to get us out there in the yard so they could smoke us down. Well, we ain't going. We'll sneak around to the back of the store and bottle 'em up. Sooner or later they'll come out.'

McCloud stepped back, raising a hand to his cheek. He said: 'It took a brave man to do that, O'Shay, holding a gun in your hand like you are.'

Some of the rest had ridden up and were crowding in through the back door. It wouldn't make any difference, Brad knew. They had not accepted him.

'All right, Rimrock,' Brad said. 'I'll do the job, me and McCloud.'

'Not me!' McCloud cried in sudden fear. 'I'm on the other side. Remember?'

'You ain't on either side,' Brad said bluntly, 'which is something you never figured out. Riley Rand don't give a damn about you if he's got your money to buy the valley. He has got it, ain't he?'

For a moment McCloud was silent, then he blurted: 'Yes, he has the money, but Gail and I are engaged to be married. That makes it different.'

Brad shook his head. 'You haven't had any experience with fellows like Riley Rand. I have. If Gail's idea of buying us out had worked, it would be different, but we didn't sell. Now Rand will bull it through his way.'

'Brad.' It was Bud Bain, calling from the front room. 'Rand's hollering at us.'

McCloud forced a laugh. 'Better go see about it, Wilder. I'm not worried.'

'You'd better be.' Turning, Brad walked to the door. He shouted: 'What's on your mind, Rand?'

'We're done waiting!' Rand called. 'Everybody that's in the house walk out or we'll burn the store.'

'We've got McCloud,' Brad said. 'If you burn the store, he's a dead duck.'

'No!' Gail screamed.

Rand's answer was a flurry of shots. Brad dropped flat on his stomach as slugs whined through the doorway.

When the echoes of the shots died, Rand called: 'We're giving you half an hour! Then the store goes. We'll burn every cabin in the valley and run your stock out. Now will you make a deal?'

'What kind of a deal?'

'We'll hold off till sundown if you'll agree to get your stuff out of the valley by then. That's the best we'll do.'

'No!' Gail screamed. 'We'll…'

She never finished. Rand, Brad guessed, had clapped his hand over her mouth.

'You boys give McCloud and me about fifteen minutes,' Brad said to those with him. 'Then throw all the slugs you can against the front of the store.'

Jeanie gripped his arm. 'What are you going to do?'

'McCloud and me will go around to the back. We'll finish this now.'

'The hell I will,' McCloud breathed. 'You're licked, and you know it.'

'No, I don't know it.' Brad motioned to O'Shay. 'You boys are sure bent on living to a ripe old age. I want to know just one thing. Will you scatter out on both sides of the house and throw some lead?'

'Yes,' O'Shay said. 'We'll do that.'

'Wait,' McCloud said. 'Wait now. Use your head. You're a long ways from any source of supplies. Suppose Riley burns the store? What will you live off?'

'Tom has a wagon of supplies coming,' Mrs Hildreth said in a low voice. 'We'll make out. Go ahead, Brad.'

He looked at her, surprised. He had thought she would be the last person in the house to say that. Perhaps it was because her husband was not here. If the fight could be finished before Tom Hildreth came, he would not be killed. It was not courage, he saw then. She was simply looking out for her man. The store meant little to her. Brad Wilder's life meant less, for if Brad were killed, there would be no more resistance.

'Don't count on that wagon,' McCloud said.

'Why not?' Mrs Hildreth demanded.

'Dollit and Nick Bailey stopped it several days ago in the mountains,' McCloud answered. 'They killed the driver and burned the wagon.'

They cried out, some of them, for they had all known Hildreth was expecting the load of supplies. Mrs Bailey lowered her head, but old Bailey drew himself erect again, desperately trying to hold onto his self-respect.

'I'll go with you, Brad,' Bailey said. 'It's too much for one man.'

'There's me and McCloud,' Brad said. 'You get back to that window. I can count on you and Jeanie and Bud Bain to throw some slugs. I ain't sure I can count on anyone else.'

'We'll do it,' O'Shay said loudly.

'I won't have no part in it,' McCloud bellowed. 'Which side do you think...?'

'You'll do it.' Brad drew his gun and lined

it on McCloud. 'Move.'

McCloud turned, and the crowd opened a path for him. They walked out, Brad a pace behind McCloud, and, when they were outside, Brad discovered that Jeanie had followed him.

She asked: 'Must it always be you, Brad?'

'I reckon,' he said. 'You hike back to the front of the house. McCloud, get down on your belly. That's the way we're travelling to the back of the store. Then you're gonna be my shield. We'll see how good you stand with Riley Rand.'

It took them ten minutes to worm their way to the rear of the store.

Brad said: 'If you want to live long enough to see the sun come up, you'd better keep quiet. They'd as soon plug you as anybody else.'

McCloud made no answer. They went on through the grass, the dawn light deepening a little. It was touch and go, and Brad knew it. He was gambling that Rand's party was in the front of the store, that Rand would not expect the fight to be brought to him. Then, thinking of the way the settlers had backed down, it seemed to Brad that Rand's judgment of the settlers had been all too accurate. Coldly realistic now, Brad knew exactly how long the odds were against him.

With time running out, he thought of Cory Steele and the faith Cory had had in him. That was the real reason he was here on his belly crawling through the grass. It was as if Cory were here with him, telling him that only a few lead but many follow, that this was a good job worth the doing, the job Cory had died for.

Brad could accept all of that now. Within these last few days he had come to believe in a new set of values. Idealistic, perhaps a little crazy, but the kind of values that made a man feel good inside, that gave the future a meaning it had never held for him before.

McCloud stopped. He said: 'Go ahead. Shoot me. I'm not going on.'

'Move,' Brad whispered. 'Damn you, move. Don't make me beef you out here like a rabbit.'

'Go ahead,' McCloud said again. 'My luck's all used up. You're right about Riley. He's got my money, and he'd just as soon kill me as not.'

Brad's face was close to McCloud's. In the thin dawn light he saw in the Easterner's expression the resignation that comes from a sense of final and utter failure.

'I'll tell you how it is,' McCloud said in a rush of words as if he wanted to say this before it was too late. 'I've been a big man's baby brother. I've had to bow and scrape and take a back seat. I wasn't man enough to play the Wall Street game, so I told my brother I'd make my own way out here. That's why I threw in with Rand.'

'Get on your feet,' Brad whispered.

But there was nothing now that could stop McCloud's flow of words. 'I love Gail. I came out here looking for a ranch and met Gail in Winnemucca. Then I met Riley and he told me he knew just the spot. I gave him the money to buy the herd and hire a crew.

I gave him more to buy the valley, but something went wrong in Salem, and the deal didn't go through. That's why we sent Dollit up here last fall. Rand said we'd come on regardless and to hell with the state. If we had the valley, they'd have to sell to us. You see how it is, Wilder. I'm not worth a damn. Not back East or out here. I had to depend on a man like Riley Rand...'

'This is no time to gab,' Brad said hotly. 'We're going through that door.'

Brad was on his feet, gun in his right hand, his left gripping McCloud's coat collar. That was when the fifteen minutes were up. Firing broke out from the house, heavy firing that came from ten or twelve Colts and Winchesters. There must have been a shotgun or two, and it sounded as if someone had grabbed Tom Hildreth's old buffalo gun off the wall and was using it.

Somehow Brad got McCloud to his feet, and he lifted a knee to the seat of the man's pants. He shouted: 'Get through that door! Damn you and your talk.' He shoved his gun muzzle into the soft fat over McCloud's ribs. 'I aimed to be going through the door when the shooting started.'

Whimpering, McCloud ran toward the door, Brad crowding behind him. The back door was locked. Brad shot the lock off and kicked the door open. The light was behind them as they crowded into the back room, and Smoke Kinnear, running in from the store, let go with a shot that knocked McCloud off his feet.

There was so little light inside the store building that Kinnear's shape was only a vague blur in front of Brad as he threw a shot at the gunman and lunged sideways out of the doorway.

'Gail!' McCloud screamed. 'Gail, he shot me! Gail! Gail...!' His last word was drowned by another report. Kinnear, coming into the back room, had shot McCloud a second time.

Gail must have followed Kinnear, for Brad saw the flash of fire from a small revolver. It was directly behind the gunman. Then the shadowy bulk of his body was gone, and Gail was running toward McCloud, screaming: 'George! Where are you, George?'

Another man loomed behind her, a squat massive shape. Whang Dollit! Brad fired and dropped behind a cracker barrel. He heard the other shoot, the slug ripping into the wall. Brad, poking his head around the barrel, caught Dollit's square body in his sights, squeezed the trigger, and saw Dollit spill forward on his face.

There was a lull in the firing from the house. Rand's gun was silent, too, but he was out there, somewhere in the front of the store.

The shooting started again. Brad thumbed shells into the cylinder of his gun and crawled forward, keeping low. Gail was behind him.

Brad reached the store and went on, hugging the floor. He could not see Rand, could not hear him. It was possible that the man had been tagged by a stray bullet, but Brad could not count on such luck. He worked his way around the end of the pine counter. Still he could not see Rand.

The minutes dragged by, each of them an eternity to Brad. He laid belly flat on the floor, gun in his right hand. The firing continued, riddling the front of the store. He moved forward again, knowing he couldn't let this go on. Gail was a potential danger behind him. Rand's nerves might crack under the pressure. If he started firing wildly and kept his bullets low, Brad was likely to stop one of them.

Then Brad's left hand, reaching forward as he crawled, touched some tools that Hildreth had left leaning against the wall. Another lull came in the firing. Brad carefully picked up a shovel and tossed it over the counter. The sound of it hitting the floor was nerve-shattering in this interlude of quiet, and it accomplished exactly what Brad wanted. Rand, hidden directly in front of Brad behind a low pile of sugar sacks, let go a shot.

Brad brought himself upright and lunged forward, firing as he moved. Now he could see Rand. His first shot must have been a clean miss, for Rand threw a bullet that seared his left side. It was the one chance Rand had, and he decreed his own death when he failed to stop Brad.

Rand was motionless, a still target, and Brad was moving. He was close now, and he shot three times, fast, and Rand thudded to the floor, gun flung from slack fingers.

'All right, all right!' Brad called. 'Hold your fire!'

They came rushing across the yard toward the store, Jeanie and old man Bailey and Bud Bain. Rimrock O'Shay was with them, talking big now that the fight was over, and Tom Hildreth was there, panting after the short run.

'I'm not hurt much,' Brad said at once in answer to Jeanie's alarmed question. 'Just lost a little meat along my ribs. Come on. Gail's back here.'

Brad ran along the counter, Jeanie a step behind him, the others trailing. O'Shay shouted: 'Rand's dead!' He stumbled over

Dollit's body, and then he saw Kinnear.

Gail was on her feet, tall and straight-backed. She said tonelessly: 'George is dead.'

Brad took her by the shoulders and shoved her through the door, saying: 'I'm sorry about McCloud, but if it hadn't been for him, this wouldn't have happened.'

She pushed Brad's hands away from her. 'I don't need your sympathy, Wilder,' she said evenly. 'Riley was right about everybody in the valley. If I had let Kinnear kill you that first night, it wouldn't have gone this way.'

'She's one of 'em,' O'Shay blurted. 'I don't see why we don't...'

'Shut up,' Brad said, 'or I'll work that ugly mug of yours over till even your own wife won't recognize you.'

O'Shay subsided at once.

Gail said: 'He'd do it, mister. You meet up with one man like Wilder in about ten million. It was our bad luck to run into him here.'

'You can go, miss,' Hildreth said. 'No one will lay a hand on you.'

'I'm to thank you, I suppose.' She looked at Jeanie, frowning. 'Well, this is justice after what happened to your father. I have no tears for my brother. This was robbery that he planned, and he deserved what he got. I tried to stop him, but I couldn't.'

'There was a letter...' Brad began.

'You'll find it in Riley's coat pocket. You own the valley, Miss Steele. You can give your people the homes your father talked about, the little people that let Brad Wilder do their fighting for them.'

She turned and would have walked away if Brad had not said: 'If you need some help...'

She swung back, angry. 'I don't need any help. Chang and I will take the wagons back down the trail. I've still got the herd. I'll find a place for it somewhere.'

This time Brad let her go. He took Jeanie's hand, and they walked toward the lake.

Jeanie said: 'You're hurt. You'd better...'

'It'll wait. I've got something to say. Been trying to say it ever since I saw you, but I got all balled up. I kept telling myself I'd wait till

I got my place to going, but I can't wait any longer. You need me and I sure need you. I always will.'

'I guess it was just as well that you waited,' she said. 'I just didn't want to grow up, but after Nick came out that time and tried to use his gun…' She paused, staring across the lake. 'Well, I knew then, Brad, I knew, and I wondered why I hadn't known all the time.'

Brad turned Jeanie to face him and kissed her, and the kiss, like the morning, was filled with promise.

'Funny,' he said softly as he put a tip of a finger against her freckled nose. 'The first time I saw you I thought you were pretty, but now you look downright beautiful.'